Nadezhda Teffi

ALL ABOUT LOVE

Translated by Darra Goldstein
Introduction by Edward J. Brown

Ardis, Ann Arbor

Nadezhda Teffi, *All about Love*
Copyright © 1985 by Ardis Publishers
All rights reserved under International and Pan-American Copyright Conventions.
Printed in the United States of America

Translated from the original Russian

Ardis Publishers
2901 Heatherway
Ann Arbor, Michigan 48104

Library of Congress Cataloging in Publication Data

Teffi, N. A., 1876-1952.
All about love.

Translation of: Vse o liubvi.
1. Teffi, N. A., 1876-1952—Translations, English.
I. Title.
PG3453.B8V713   1985   891.73'42   85-7395
ISBN 0-88233-792-0 (alk. paper)

For Bertram and Ella Wolfe

Contents

Introduction by Edward J. Brown   9
Flirting   13
Time   23
The Fairy Karabos   29
Insurance   35
Two Diaries   41
The Nightmare   47
About Eternal Love   53
The Suitor   59
Mr. Furtenau's Cat   65
Don Quixote and the Turgenevan Girl   71
Two Affairs with Foreigners   77
The Choice of a Cross   87
Points of View   95
A Banal Story   101
A Psychological Fact   107
The Gentleman   113
The Wonder of Spring   119
The Dear Departed   125
A Woman's Lot   131
An Atmosphere of Love   137
An Easter Story   143
The Shopgirl's Tale   149
A Wise Man   153
The Magpie   159
Secret Hiding Places Revealed   165
A Bright Life   171
Scoundrels   172
A Virtuoso of Feeling   187
What We Weren't Told About Faust   191
Iago   197

A Salubrious Art

The short stories and sketches signed by the pen name Teffi (Nadezhda Alexandrovna Lokhvitskaya, 1872-1952) enjoyed immense popularity in Russia before the Revolution, and after the author's emigration to Paris in 1919 her regular contributions to Russian emigre newspapers had a large and devoted readership. Most of her work was published first in various ephemeral media and offered to her public as brief, amusing commentary on absurdities of character and situation. That work itself is anything but ephemeral, and Gleb Struve's judgment that Teffi's newspaper sketches were genuine literature, perhaps surprising when it was offered many years ago, has been confirmed in the experience of contemporary readers. There is a strain of the tragic in her pictures of ridiculous humans fumbling their opportunities for sex or love or glory, and the old Russian cliche "laughter through tears" (or "tears through laughter" —why not?) can be avoided in discussing her only with difficulty. But Teffi's work eludes cliches and stands as unique among the Russian satirical humorists with whom she is often compared: Chekhov (Chekhonte!), Averchenko, Zoshchenko. The brief misadventures she recounts take place, in the main, among Russian emigres settled in Paris: former aristocrats, former rich men, former intelligentsia, and former simple Russian folk living out a sad life amid the alien corn. Yet the final effect of her writing upon the reader is not, paradoxically, one of sadness at a tragic human fate, but rather a kind of elation at the unpremeditated power of her laconic Russian and repeated surprise at her simple, neat narrative arrangements. In her stories art triumphs over material and enriches our life, and no doubt in her own life the practice of her craft made a miserable existence almost bearable. Thus in the story "Time" the narrative of old Maria Nikolaevna's wild adventures as an irresistible young beauty frames her fat old face, powdered, rouged, and featuring expensive false teeth, and suspends for one beautiful moment the ugly work of time itself. Teffi's verbal art is almost always like that.

Professor Goldstein is to be congratulated on having produced a lucid and sensitive version of one of Teffi's most characteristic collections. The English-speaking reader will be happy to make the acquaintance of a Russian writer who deserves her own place in the Pantheon.

Edward J. Brown

Acknowledgements

I would like to thank Edward J. Brown for his encouragement, advice, and continued interest in this project and my husband, Dean Crawford, for his intrepid editorial work.

Flirting

The cabin was unbearably stuffy. It smelled of a scorched iron and hot oilcloth. Platonov could not raise the blind because the window looked out onto the deck, and so, in the dark, irritated and in a hurry, he was shaving and changing his clothes.

"As soon as the steamer starts moving it'll be cooler," he consoled himself. "The train wasn't really any better."

He spruced himself up in a bright suit and white shoes, and after carefully combing his dark hair, thinning on the crown of his head, he went out onto the deck. It was easier to breathe here, but the deck was burning from the sun, and not the slightest movement of air could be felt, even though the steamer was already quivering, and the gardens and belltowers of the mountainous shore, slowly turning, were drifting off into the distance.

"We're off!"

It was a bad time of year on the Volga. The end of July. The river was already growing shallow and the steamers proceeded slowly, taking soundings as they went.

Surprisingly few passengers were in first class: a huge fat merchant in a visored cap with his old and quiet wife, a priest, two discontented elderly ladies.

Platonov strode up and down the steamer several times. "Pretty dull!"

Although, in the light of certain circumstances, it was very convenient. More than anything, Platonov was afraid of meeting people he knew.

"But still, why is the ship so empty?"

Suddenly, a rollicking nightclub tune resounded from the steamer's salon, and a somewhat hoarse baritone began singing to the accompaniment of a jangly piano. Platonov smiled and gravitated toward these pleasant sounds.

The salon was empty save for a thickset young man in a light blue chintz Russian blouse, sitting at the piano, which was decorated with a bouquet of colored feather-grass. He sat sideways on a stool like a coachman on his box, his left knee lowered towards the floor and his elbows spread dashingly. In coachman fashion too, as if he were driving a troika, he was thrashing along the keys.

> "A bit of a touch-me-not is this girl,
> Somewhat aloof, not seeking a whirl,
> Her very coolness lures him on . . ."

He shook his mighty mane of light, badly combed hair.

> "And then the sweet lasses
> Will let him make passes,
> And trala-la-la-la
> And trala-la."

He noticed Platonov and jumped up. "Allow me to introduce myself. Okulov, medical student of cholera."

"Ah, yes." Platonov understood. "That's why there are so few passengers. Cholera."

"Cholera? What the hell kind of cholera are you talking about? These people get drunk... and they throw up. I've rushed around on a million trips already and I still haven't verified even a single case of cholera."

This student Okulov had a healthy red face, darker than his hair, and his expression was like that of a person about to punch someone in the nose: mouth stretched in a grimace, nostrils flared, eyes bulging. As if nature had frozen that final moment before the blow, then let the student just go like that his whole life long.

"Yes, old man," continued the student. "Utter and absolute boredom. Not a single female. And if one does get on the boat, she'll have such an ugly kisser it'll make you seasick on the calmest water. But what about you, are you travelling for pleasure? It's not worth it. The river's a lot of crap. It's hot and smelly. You hear all kinds of swearing at the docks. The captain—who the hell knows what *he's* up to—he must be a dipsomaniac, he doesn't drink vodka at the table. His wife is just a girl—been married four months. I was gonna try to talk with her, just as though she had some sense. Such a fool, a real pain in the ass. Thought she could teach me something. 'Lead me among those who perish for the great cause of Love!' 'Do good for the people!'* What a bossy broad. Have you ever seen such a girl—comes from Vyatka** with spiritual interests and intuitive subtleties. I said to hell with her and left. By the way, do you know this tune? It's great:

---

*The first quote is from Nikolai Nekrasov's poem "Knight for an Hour" (1862). The complete line is as follows: "Away from the exultant, idly prating,/Who stain their hands with blood,/Lead me among those who perish/For the great cause of love!" The second quote is simply a slogan. (Trans.)

**Vyatka, the present-day Kirov, is situated in the hinterlands of Russia and it is the butt of many jokes. Okulov implies that the girl, coming from Vyatka, could not possibly have "spiritual interests." (Trans.)

Flirting

'There's a delightful aroma
From my flowers . . .'

They sing it in every nightclub." He quickly turned around, sat again on the "coachman's box," shook his dishevelled hair, and started to sing:

"Alas, mama,
Ach, what is this . . ."

"And that's a medical student?" thought Platonov as he left to wander along the deck.

****

The passengers dragged themselves to dinner: that same merchant mastodon with his wife, the tiresome old women, the priest, two other tradesmen, and a person with long, stringy hair, dirty underwear, a copper pince-nez, and newspapers in his bulging pockets.

They ate on the deck, each at his own little table. Even the captain came—gray, puffy and gloomy, wearing a shabby sackcloth uniform jacket. With him a girl of about fourteen with slicked-down hair, a braid curled at the end, and a chintz frock.

Platonov had already finished his traditional cold fish and vegetable soup when the medical student approached his table and called to the waiter: "Set my place over here!"

"Certainly, certainly!" Platonov invited him. "Glad to have you."

The medical student sat down. He asked for vodka and herring.

"A wre-etched river!" he began the conversation. "'Oh Volga, Volga, with your high waters in spring, you don't flood the meadows the way you should . . .'* Not the way you should. The Russian intellectual is always giving some kind of lesson or other. The Volga, he says, doesn't flood the way it should. He knows how to flood better than it does."

"Wait a minute," Platonov interjected. "I think you've got it mixed up. Never mind, though. I don't remember exactly how it goes, either."

"Neither do I," the student goodnaturedly agreed. "Did you ever see our little fool?"

---

*This line is a misquotation from Nikolai Nekrasov's poem "Reflections at the Front Door" (1858).

"What little fool?"

"The bossy female. There, sitting with the captain. Not looking this way on purpose. Indignant at my 'nightclub nature.' "

"What?" Platonov was surprised. "That girl? She couldn't be more than fifteen."

"No, a little older. Maybe seventeen. And is he good looking? I said to her, 'You know, it's the same as marrying a woodchuck. How could the priest have agreed to marry you?' Ha-ha! A woodchuck with a wisp of a girl! So what do you think? She was offended! The little fool!"

****

The evening was quiet and pink. The colored lanterns on the buoys flamed up, and magically, sleepily, the steamer slipped between them. The passengers dispersed early to their cabins. Only on the lower deck the carpenters, crowded together, still busied themselves sawing wood, while a Tatar droned a song like a mosquito.

Nearby, a light, white shawl, stirred by the breeze, attracted Platonov.

The small figure of the captain's wife clung to the side of the ship and did not move.

"Dreaming?" asked Platonov.

She started and turned around, frightened.

"Oh! I thought it was that . . ."

"That medical student? Hm? A pretty vulgar type."

Then she turned her gentle, thin little face to him, gazing up with huge eyes whose color it was hard to discern.

Platonov spoke in a serious tone, inspiring confidence. He severely condemned the medical student for his nightclub tunes. He even expressed surprise that such vulgarities could occupy him, whom fate had given the opportunity to serve the holy cause of bringing aid to suffering mankind.

The captain's little wife now turned her whole body to him, like a flower to the sun, and even opened her little mouth.

The moon came out, still new. It did not shine brightly yet, but simply hung in the sky like a decoration. The plashing of the river was barely audible. The forests on the mountainous shore were growing dark. It was quiet.

Platonov did not want to go into his stuffy cabin, and in order to keep this sweet, faintly illuminated nighttime face near to him, he kept on talking, talking about the loftiest topics, sometimes even embarrassing himself. "What a lot of bunk!" he said to himself.

Flirting

Dawn was already turning pink when, sleepy and pleasantly excited, he went to bed.

****

The next day was that fatal 23rd of July, when—for only a few hours, for just one night—she, Vera Petrovna, was supposed to board the steamer.

Regarding this rendezvous, planned last spring, Platonov had already received a dozen letters and telegrams. He had to coordinate his business trip to Saratov with her pleasure trip to friends at their estate. They imagined a wonderful, poetic meeting, which no one would ever find out about. Vera Petrovna's husband was busy with the construction of a distillery and could not accompany her. Everything was going as easy as pie.

The upcoming rendezvous did not worry Platonov. He hadn't seen Vera Petrovna for three months already, and that's a long time in the life of an affair. You tend to forget. But still, the meeting promised to be pleasant, a diversion, a break between complicated Petersburg affairs and the unpleasant business meetings awaiting him in Saratov.

To pass the time, he lay down to sleep right after breakfast and slept till about five o'clock. Then he very carefully combed his hair, rubbed himself all over with eau de cologne, cleaned up his cabin—just in case—and went out onto the deck to inquire: wouldn't they be reaching that fateful dock soon? He remembered the captain's wife, glanced around for her but didn't find her. Well, he had no use for her now anyway.

A carriage stood at the small dock. Some gentlemen and a lady in a white dress were bustling about.

Platonov decided it would be more prudent to stay out of sight—just in case. Maybe her husband was seeing her off.

He went behind a smokestack and came out when the dock had already disappeared from view.

"Arkady Nikolaevich!"

"Darling!"

Vera Petrovna was red-faced, her hair clinging to her forehead. "Eleven miles in this heat!" Breathing heavily from excitement, she squeezed his hand.

"This is madness . . . madness . . ." he kept repeating, not knowing what to say.

And suddenly, right behind his back, the joyful cry of an unpleasantly familiar voice was heard: "Auntie! What a surprise! Where are you going?" the cholera student cried out. He brushed

Platonov with his shoulder and, pressing upon the perplexed lady, gave her a smacking kiss on the cheek.

"This is... allow me to introduce..." she began to babble with an expression of hopeless despair. "This is my husband's nephew, Vasya Okulov."

"We already know each other very well." The student was cheerfully enjoying the situation. "And do you know, Auntie, you got terribly fat in the country! My God! Look at that midriff! A real monument!"

"Ach, stop that!" Vera Petrovna cried, almost in tears.

"I didn't know you knew each other!" The student continued to enjoy himself. "Maybe you've met on purpose? A rendezvous? Ha-ha-ha! Let's go, Auntie, I'll show you to your cabin. Goodbye, Monsieur Platonov. Shall we all dine *ensemble?*"

Vasya did not fall even a step behind poor Vera Petrovna the whole evening. Only during dinner did the bright idea come to him of going by himself into the bar to raise hell about the warm vodka. Those few minutes were hardly enough for them to express their despair and their love and their hope that maybe the bastard would calm down during the night.

"When everyone has fallen asleep, come up onto the deck, to the smokestack, I'll be waiting," whispered Platonov.

"Only for God's sake, be more careful! He might tell my husband on us."

The evening passed very tediously. Vera Petrovna was nervous. Platonov was irritated, and both of them constantly tried in their conversation to let the student know that they had met quite by chance and were very surprised at this circumstance.

The student was having a great time, singing idiotic couplets and feeling himself to be the life of the party.

"Well, and now to bed, to bed, to bed!" he ordered. "Tomorrow you must get up early, there's no point tiring yourself out. I'm responsible to Uncle for you."

Vera Petrovna pressed Platonov's hand significantly as she left, escorted by her nephew.

A slight shadow slipped past near the rail. A quiet little voice called out. Platonov quickly turned away and walked off towards his cabin.

"Now that one is going to hang onto me, too," he thought about the captain's little wife.

After waiting half an hour, he very quietly went out onto the deck and made for the smokestack.

"Is it you?"

"It's me."

Flirting

She was already waiting for him, looking prettier in the foggy twilight, wrapped up in a long dark veil.

"Vera Petrovna! Darling! How terrible!"

"This is terrible! Terrible!" she whispered. "How hard it was to persuade my husband. He didn't want me to go alone to the Severyakov's, he's jealous of Mishka. He wanted to go in June, I pretended to be sick. Everything was altogether difficult, such a trial..."

"Listen, Vera, darling! Let's go to my cabin. It'll be safer there, really. We'll sit very, very quietly, we'll leave the lights out. I'll just kiss your dear little eyes, just listen to your voice. After all, for all these months I've heard it only in my dreams. Your voice! Is it really possible to forget it! Vera! Say something to me!"

"Ah-ha!" a somewhat hoarse baritone voice exclaimed above them.

Vera Petrovna quickly jumped off to the side.

"What's going on here?" continued the student because, of course, it was he. "It's foggy and damp, and you know you can sit out on the river too long at night. Tsk-tsk-tsk. Such an auntie! I'll write and tell Uncle everything. To bed, to bed, to bed! Arkady Nikolaevich, chase her off to bed. No arguments. She'll chill her stomach and catch cholera."

"I'm going, I'm going," Vera Petrovna mumbled in a tremulous voice.

"Taking such risks!" The student did not calm down. "Damp, fog!"

"What business is it of yours?" Platonov grew angry.

"What do you mean? It is I who is responsible to Uncle for her. And it's late. To bed, to bed, to bed. I'll escort you, Auntie, and stand watch all night at your door, lest you pop out again and catch a chill."

****

In the morning, after a very cold goodbye, Vera Petrovna left the steamer.

In the evening, a slight figure in a bright frock approached Platonov.

"Are you sad?" she asked.

"No. Why do you think so?"

"Well, why wouldn't you be... your Vera Petrovna left." Her voice rang out unexpectedly boldly, like a challenge.

Platonov began to laugh. "You know, she's the aunt of your friend, the cholera student. She even resembles him—didn't you notice?"

And suddenly she began to laugh, so trustingly, like a child, that he himself became lighthearted and gay. And it was as if this laughter made them friends right away, and they carried on heart-to-heart conversations. Platonov learned that the captain was a fine person and had promised to let her go to Moscow in the fall to study.

"No, don't go to Moscow!" Platonov interrupted her. "Go to Petersburg."

"Why?"

"What do you mean, why? Because I'm there!"

And she took his hand with her thin little hands and laughed with happiness.

The night was altogether wonderful. At dawn a dirty figure came out from behind the smokestack and yawning, called: "Marusyonok, my little night owl! It's time to sleep."

It was the captain.

They spent one more night on the deck. The waxing moon showed Platonov Marusenka's huge eyes, inspired and clear.

"Don't forget my telephone number," he said to these delightful eyes. "You don't even have to give your name. I'll recognize you by your voice."

"Really? Impossible!" she whispered rapturously. "Will you really recognize it?"

"You'll see! How could I forget it, your gentle little voice! Just say 'It's me.'"

And what a wonderful life would begin after this call! Theater—the most serious, of course—and scholarly lectures, exhibitions. Art has tremendous significance . . . And so does beauty. For example, her beauty . . .

And she listened! How she listened! And when something struck her very much, she said "Really!" so fondly, so dearly.

Early in the morning he got off at Saratov. His boring business acquaintances were already waiting for him at the dock. They made unnaturally friendly faces. Platonov thought that one of these friendly faces would be convicted of embezzlement, the other driven out for idleness. Already worried and angry, he began to descend the ladder. Turning around by chance, he caught sight of *her* at the rail. She screwed up her sleepy little face and firmly pressed her lips together, as if afraid of bursting into tears, but her eyes shone so huge and happy, that he involuntarily smiled at them.

****

In Saratov the days overflowed with business, the nights with drunken revelry. In Ochkin's nightclub, famous along the whole

Flirting

Volga for its merchant drinking bouts, Platonov, as happens, had to spend a night with his business colleagues. There were groups of singers—gypsy, Hungarian, Russian. A distinguished Volga merchant was bullying a waiter who accidentally had spilled some champagne on the tablecloth while pouring out forty-eight glasses.

"You can't even pour, you son of a bitch!" The merchant tore at the tablecloth, smashing the glasses into smithereens. The rug and armchairs were flooded with champagne. "Try it again!"

The smell of wine, the cigar smoke, the hubbub.

"*Rytka! Rytka!*" the Hungarian girls sang in their hoarse, sleepy voices.

At dawn a kind of wild howling, quite like a flock of sheep, could be heard in the adjoining room.

"What the hell is that?"

"It's Mr. Apollosov having a grand time. Towards the end he always gathers all the waiters together and makes them sing."

The story went that this Apollosov, a modest country schoolteacher, bought a winning ticket in installments from Heinrich Blok and won 75,000 roubles. And as soon as he got the money, he just settled in a Ochkin's. Now his capital was running out. He still wanted to spend it here at the club, up to his last kopeck. That was his dream. Then he would ask for his former position again, live out his life as a country schoolteacher, and always remember that luxurious time when the waiters sang to him in unison at the break of day.

Well, where besides Russia and in the soul of a Russian can you find such bliss?

****

Autumn passed. The cold set in.

Winter began in a complicated way for Platonov, with various unpleasant events in his business dealings. He had to work long hours, and the work was nerve-wracking, disturbing, and crucial.

One day he was sitting in his study, expecting an important visitor. The telephone rang.

"Who's speaking?"

"It's me!" a female voice joyfully answered. "Me! Me!"

"Who's 'me'?" Platonov asked with irritation. "Excuse me, I'm very busy."

"Yes—me! It's—me!" the voice answered again and added, as if surprised: "Don't you recognize my voice? It's—me."

"My good woman," Platonov said with vexation. "I assure you that I have absolutely no time now to occupy myself with riddles. I'm very busy. Please speak to the point."

"That means you didn't recognize my voice?" the girl asked in despair.

"Oh!" Platonov figured it out. "Well, what do you mean, of course I recognized it. Could I really fail to recognize your dear little voice, Vera Petrovna!"

Silence. And then softly, sadly: "Vera Petrovna? Really . . . If that's how it is, then never mind . . . I don't need a thing . . ."

Suddenly he remembered: It's the little one! The little one on the Volga! Good Lord, what have I done! To hurt the little one like that!

"I recognized it! I recognized it!" he cried into the receiver, surprised at both his joy and his despair. "For God's sake! I really did recognize it!"

But there was no reply.

Time

The restaurant was a good one, offering shashlik, pelmeni, suckling pig, sturgeon, and a program of entertainment. The music was not limited solely to Russian favorites like "Little Bast Sandals," "Little Rolls," and "Dark Eyes." Among the performers were Negroes, Mexicans, Spaniards, and gentlemen of an indeterminable jazz tribe, who sang barely intelligible, nasal words in every language, while rocking their hips. Even the obviously Russian performers, after crossing themselves backstage, would consent to sing encores in French and in English.

The dance numbers—in which the performers were able to keep their nationalities hidden—were performed by ladies with the most exotic names: Takuza Iyuka, Rutuf Yai-yai, Ekama Yuya.

Among the performers were dark, almost black women with long green eyes. There were also rosy-gold blondes and fiery red ones with brown skin. Almost all of them, up to and including the mulattoes were, of course, Russian. What with our native talent, even this diversity isn't hard to achieve; we take strange forms by necessity. After all, "Poverty is Our Sister," and she's taught us all kinds of things.

The decor of the restaurant was chic. This word describes it best of all. Not luxurious, not sumptuous, not refined, just chic—the colored lampshades, the small fountains, the green aquariums with gold fish set into the walls, the rugs, the ceiling painted with unintelligible designs (among which you could detect a bulging eye or an uplifted leg, a pineapple, or a piece of nose with a monocle attached, or a crayfish tail). To the clientele it seemed that all these objects were falling down onto their heads, but apparently, this was precisely the effect intended by the artist.

The waiters were polite and did not say to tardy guests: "Wait a bit. Why are you shoving when there're no seats? This ain't a trolley, you know."

The restaurant was frequented by as many foreigners as Russians. You could often see some Frenchman or Englishman who had obviously visited this establishment before and had now returned, bringing his friends along with him. This same foreigner, with the expression of a magician swallowing burning oakum, would chug down his first glass of vodka, and then opening his eyes wide, cork the vodka in his throat with a *pirozhok*.* His friends would look at him

---

*The Russian word for "meat pie." The plural is *pirozhki*, with the stress on the final syllable. (Trans.)

as if he were a fearless eccentric, and smiling mistrustfully, sniff at their own glasses.

The French love to order *pirozhki*. For some reason they're amused by this word, which they pronounce with the stress on the 'o.' This is a very strange habit which can't be explained. With all Russian words, the French stress the final syllable, as they would in their own language. That is, with all Russian words except *pirozhki*.

****

Vava von Merzen, Musya Riven and Gogosya Livensky were sitting at one of the tables. Gogosya was from the uppermost circle of society, though he was only peripherally connected; and so, in spite of his sixty-five years, he was still called by his nickname, Gogosya.

Vava von Merzen, who was actually an aging Varvara, had twisted, dry curls the color of tobacco smoked so thoroughly that if they were cut off and finely chopped, they could be used to stuff the pipe of some undiscriminating seafarer.

Musya Riven was a young miss, just divorced for the first time. She was sad, sentimental and tender, but this did not stop her from downing glass after glass of vodka, all to no effect. No one, including Musya herself, paid the least attention.

Gogosya was a fascinating conversationalist. He knew everyone and gossiped about them in a booming voice. In the juiciest parts of his conversation he would switch over to French—as is the Russian custom—partly so that the "waiters wouldn't understand," and partly because French indecencies are piquant, while Russian improprieties offend the ear.

Gogosya knew exactly what should be ordered at any restaurant. He shook hands with the maître d's, knew each cook by name, and always remembered what he had dined on, when and where. He would loudly applaud a successful act and cry out in a low, lordly voice: "Thank you, brother!" or: "Well done, tootsie!" He knew many of the clientele and made each a welcoming gesture, sometimes roaring across the whole hall: "*Comment ça va?* Is Anna Petrovna *en bonne santé?*" All in all, he was a marvelous customer, filling the hall three-quarters full with his presence alone.

An interesting party occupied the small table across from them, against the other wall. Three women. All three were more than elderly. Plainly speaking, they were ancient.

A small, thickset woman, whose head was screwed right into her bust without any hint of a neck whatsoever, was directing the whole affair. A large diamond brooch was wedged against her double chin. Her grey, coiffed hair was covered with a coquettish little black hat, her cheeks were encased in pinkish powder, and her very modestly made-up mouth revealed porcelain teeth of a bluish cast. A magnificent silver fox stole fluffed up higher than her ears. The old woman was the height of elegance.

The other two were less interesting and had obviously been invited by the well-dressed old woman.

She chose both the wine and the food painstakingly. Meanwhile her guests, evidently knowing which side their bread was buttered on, emphatically expressed and defended their own selections. They all began to eat at the same time and with gusto, drinking knowledgeably and with concentration. They quickly became flushed. The leading lady, the one the others looked to for approval, even turned a little blue. Her eyes bulged, bloodshot and glassy. But all three were in a joyful, excited mood, like tribesmen who have just skinned an elephant—that time when joy demands a continuation of the dance, but satiation drags them to the ground.

"Amusing old women!" said Vava von Merzen, directing her lorgnette at the merry party.

"Yes!" Gogosya replied enthusiastically. "A happy age. They no longer need to keep up their figures, they don't have to try to catch anyone or appeal to anyone. With money and good digestion it's the happiest time of life. And the most carefree. You no longer have to construct your life. Everything is finished."

"Look at that old bird, the dominant one," said Musya Riven, scornfully curling the corners of her mouth. "Just like some kind of contented cow. I can tell what she's been like her whole life long."

"She's probably lived it up," said Gogosya approvingly. "Live and let live, Musya. She's merry, healthy, and rich. Maybe she wasn't even too bad-looking in her day. Of course it's hard to judge now, when a lump of pink fat is all that remains . . ."

"I think she was stingy, greedy and dumb," Vava von Merzen interjected. "Look how she gobbles and slurps, the animal."

"But all the same, someone probably loved her, and even married her," Musya Riven drawled dreamily on.

"Someone married her only for her money. You're always imagining romance where it doesn't exist."

Tula Rovtsyn interrupted the conversation. He was from the same fringe of society as Gogosya and for that reason kept the name Tula even though he was sixty-three. Tula was also well-mannered and pleasant, but poorer than Gogosya and much gloomier. After chatting for several minutes he straightened up again, glanced around, and went up to the vivacious old women. They were as pleased to see him as an old friend, and asked him to join them at their table.

Meanwhile, the program continued.

A young man came out onto the stage, licked his lips like a cat who's eaten a chicken, and to the accompaniment of howling and the intermittent jangling of jazz, he performed an English song, crooning imploringly like a woman. The words of the song were sentimental and even sad, the tune monotonously melancholy, but the jazz did its own thing without investigating such details. The effect was as though a sad old gentleman were tearfully recounting his amorous misadventures while some maniac leapt wildly about, howling and whistling and beating the tearful gentleman on the head with a brass tray.

Then two Spanish girls danced to the same music. One of them screamed as she ran off the stage, which greatly heightened the mood of the audience.

Afterwards a Russian singer with a French name appeared. First he sang a French love song, then, for an encore, an old Russian melody:

> "Your humble slave, I kneel,
> Not struggling with my fate.
> I'm well prepared to meet the shame I'll feel—
> All for the joy of you as my mate!"

"Listen! Listen!" Gogosya suddenly pricked up his ears. "Ah, what memories! What a terrible tragedy that love song evokes! Poor Kolya Izubov . . . Maria Nikolaevna Rutte . . . the Count . . ."

> "When my gaze meets your eyes
> I'm seized by ecstasy . . ."

the singer languidly crooned.

"I knew them all," Gogosya recalled. "Kolya Izubov wrote that song. Charming music. He was very talented. A sailor . . ."

> "And mirrored are starry skies
> In the deep and stormy sea . . ."

the singer continued.

"How charming she was, Maria Nikolaevna. Both Kolya and the Count were in love with her, like madmen. Kolya challenged the Count to a duel, and the Count killed him. Maria Nikolaevna's husband was in the Caucasus at the time. He returns, and here's this

Time

scandal and Maria Nikolaevna nursing the dying Kolya. The Count, seeing Maria Nikolaevna constantly at Kolya's side, shoots himself in the forehead, leaving her a letter saying he knew of her true love for Kolya. The letter, of course, falls into the husband's hands, and he demands a divorce. Maria Nikolaevna loves him passionately and is guilty of no more than beauty and kindness. But Rutte doesn't believe her. He accepts a position in the Far East and leaves her. She is in despair, suffers dreadfully, tries to enter a convent. After six years her husband calls her to him in Shanghai. She flies there, restored to life. But she finds him dying. They spent only two months together. He finally understood everything—the whole time he had loved only her and was tormented. It was such a tragedy that you're amazed how this little woman could live through it all. I lost track of her after that. All I heard was that she married again, and her husband was killed in the war. I think she may have died, too, killed during the Revolution. Tula here knew her well, even suffered in his time."

". . . the deep and sto-o-rmy sea."

"A remarkable woman! You don't find that kind anymore."
Offended, Vava von Merzen and Musya Riven remained silent.
"There are interesting women in every era," Vava von Merzen finally said in a strained voice.
But Gogosya only patted her hand sarcastically and good-naturedly.
"Look," said Musya, "your friend is talking about you with his old women."
Tula and the ladies were, in fact, looking right at Gogosya. Tula stood up and came over to his friend, and the leading lady motioned with her head.
"Gogosya!" said Tula. "It turns out that Maria Nikolaevna remembers you well. I only told her your first name, and immediately she remembered you and is very happy to see you again."
"Which Maria Nikolaevna?" Gogosya was taken aback.
"Negolina. The former Rutte. Have you really forgotten?"
"Oh my God! I was just talking about her! Where is she?"
"Let's join her for a minute," Tula hurried on. "I'm sure your dear ladies will excuse you."
Gogosya jumped up, looking round in surprise.
"Where is she?"
"Over there, I was just sitting with her . . . I'll take you right to her!" he cried.

27

The leading lady motioned again to Gogosya with her head. And affably moving apart her firm fat cheeks with her lipsticked mouth, she flashed him a perfect row of blue porcelain teeth.

The Fairy Karabos

Two days in a row the cook, Aksinya, came running to Ilka.

Aksinya was strong, with a dark, ruddy complexion and teeth so white that from a distance she seemed to be holding a piece of curd cheese in her mouth.

She came running to Ilka in hopes of being hired as a nanny for their expected child.

Ilka was pleased that Aksinya was so cheerful and daring and called herself "Senka" like a country boy.

Senka spoke in a secret whisper, constantly glancing at the door—maybe someone was eavesdropping! But then she would laugh at the top of her lungs. "If you have a son, ma'am, I'll sew a little cap for him. One side will be red, the other yellow. Ha-ha-ha! And if it's a daughter, she'll need a cap with lace." The last time Senka visited, she talked such bright nonsense that even the unhappy Ilka cheered up. Senka told her about a certain German who had a goat with a red woolen harness and bells around its neck. The bells were not like horse bells, though. These were small and gold and they simply sang! Senka wanted to cut a bell or two off the goat's harness to put away for the little one: "We'll tie them onto a little rope. He'll strum it with his hands and be merry the rest of his life. You can't buy bells like that in town, you know. They're obviously imported. It won't do any harm to cut one off, they'll never notice. And even if they did, they won't know who did it. Ha-ha-ha!"

Senka was silly and cunning, yet she made life so simple and merry that you wouldn't want to part with her for anything. But there was a serious obstacle in the way of Ilka's happiness with Senka. In Senka's past hovered two children without a single husband. One child had died in the village, the other was "maybe alive." Ilka's sullen husband, Stanya, refused to hire Senka.

Ilka was planning to make up a story portraying Senka as a victim, but somehow she didn't know how to begin. At the very thought of a conversation with Stanya, her heart began to pound.

But one day he himself began to speak: "We have to find a nanny for our new baby."

Ilka became nervous. She gasped for breath and prepared to speak, but Stanya continued talking. "I've had luck," he said triumphantly. "I've found a governess for the child. She's the sister of the druggist's wife. She herself can't have children, so she's ready to sacrifice her life to the interests of someone else's child."

"Good Lord!" thought Ilka. "How dreadfully he's talking! What kind of interests does a small child have? How depressing, how terrible life can seem!"

"This woman's, or rather, this spinster's name is Kazimira Karlovna. She's never been employed before. This will be her first job here with us. And what's especially valuable is the fact that she's hunchbacked."

Ilka paled. "Valuable?" she repeated softly.

"Yes, valuable," Stanya said, stubbornly thrusting his forehead forward. "You can't understand that, of course, although now that you're preparing for motherhood, you should apply yourself to your responsibilities with more sensitivity." He began to smoke a cigarette and swing his knee.

"He's angry!" thought Ilka. "But why?"

"The child should learn from the very first days of his life to love everything unfortunate. He will become attached to his deformed governess—luckily, she's ugly, too, quite apart from her offensive shape—and he will suffer along with her from the jabs and derision of the vulgar crowd. This woman, or rather, this spinster, has already set the condition that we don't force her to walk the child in the park. Instead, every day she will take the child in his carriage to the cemetery, where she has acquired a site for her grave. I find that a splendid idea. If they walk in the park, the passersby will 'ooh' and 'ah' in delight over the child, implanting vanity into his young soul. What's the point of that? And she's also demanded that no guests be allowed in the nursery. Not to show the child to anyone. Yes. Here again, it's no doubt unpleasant for her to catch their scornful glances."

"I don't understand a thing," Ilka said, flushing. "Why these 'scornful glances' all of a sudden? Whoever laughs at hunchbacks?"

Everyone does!" her husband cut her off. "You in the first place. Even if you don't laugh at them, you certainly don't approve. Deny it if you can, madame."

Ilka began to cry. "I can't understand your desire to surround the child with deformity and suffering. What for? Why torment him? What is he, an escaped convict or something? Maybe he'll turn out to be kind and compassionate of his own accord."

"The saints slept with lepers!" Stanya said darkly.

"Now you're going to look for a leprous nanny!" Ilka cried in despair. "You shove these lepers off on me every time. No, if I were a saint, I wouldn't lie down to sleep with a leper. I would give him my bed, but I myself would leave the room. A leper needs his rest and comfort. Instead, what does he get? He has to huddle up close to the wall, while next to him some bearded saint snores, emphasizing his self-sacrifice! That's no good. It's not the leper he loves, but himself. It's not the leper he cares about. He only wants to overcome his own revulsion in the name of self-perfection. No, I won't give my child to a leper. You yourself can go lie down with them."

Ilka jumped up, crying and stumbling against the chairs and the doorframe. She went to her room to lie down and soon dozed off. Out in the yard, little bells began to ring, not horses' bells, but fine, sharp ones—probably the goat's bells, those the jolly Senka had stolen for the child. The little bells began to ring, then terrible wheels began to rumble. And suddenly a squeak, a yelp. In her dream, Ilka got up, stole over to the window and peered out. She saw an enormous wagon, with rear wheels twice as large as the front, bound thickly with iron. In front of the wagon huge rats were rolling around, rolling over from stomach onto back. Soft and fat, they got tangled in the red traces and squealed. Then out of the wagon, reaching for the step with a bony old leg, climbed the terrible, long-nosed hunchback, the evil fairy Karabos. Her nose had grown large enough for two, and it was crooked besides. Her hump was narrow and high, and it shook with every step.

"It's the nanny for our little one," thought Ilka and shuddered all over. "She'll take the little one to sleep with lepers."

The hunchback Karabos stopped, craned her neck and groped with her eyes along the windows, looking for Ilka. Ilka thought, "If she finds me, she'll prick me with her eye, and it will be the end, it will be my ruin."

Ilka covered her face with her hands and screamed and screamed. Her screams woke her up.

She was drenched and altogether weakened. It must be a fever.

****

The doctor came the next day. Not the one who always came—he'd gone on vacation for a month—but his substitute, young and dark, with white teeth like Senka's. He felt Ilka's pulse and shook his head.

"Anemia. What are you always worrying about? Afraid of having a baby? That's nonsense, you know."

"She has a bad character," Stanya broke in. "Here I managed to find a governess for the child—it's not an easy task, you know. But *she* . . ." He turned to address his wife: "Incidentally, I saw her, and she added to her conditions. She doesn't want you to go into the nursery at night."

"Why not?"

"It will obviously embarrass her."

"The fairy Karabos unscrews her coffin at night and turns into a rat," Ilka murmured thoughtfully.

The doctor listened, frowning. He didn't understand a thing.

"Who is this governess?"

"Kazimira Karlovna, the sister of the druggist's wife."

"Are you crazy?" the doctor began to shout. "You want to take that witch into your home? I know what she's like. I treated the druggist's wife. Not a single cook can get along with her. She's positively a witch. What do you need her for?"

"I want the child to learn from the first days of his life to love all unfortunate, ugly, and wretched people."

"Ha-ha-ha!" the doctor flashed his white teeth. "Look at him! And for himself he chose a young and pretty wife!"

Ilka blushed so furiously that her ears began to ring.

Stanya only smirked. "Frankly speaking, I never considered my present wife either beautiful or intelligent."

"Did you marry her for her money then?" the doctor asked.

"No," Ilka's husband answered with forced calmness. "She didn't have any money. I married her because it seemed to me that her soul presented certain raw materials, from which it would be possible to mold a um . . . person, as I conceive of one."

"Aha," said the doctor, his eyes beginning to twinkle. "That means you married raw material." And he burst out laughing. "You've entangled yourself in hypocrisy, my friend. Now don't get angry at me for talking like this, but you're really very funny!"

Stanya slowly began to smoke, emphasizing his composure. "Of course," he said, "you as a doctor, as a physiologist, attach little significance to the cultivation of the spirit. The saints shared their beds with lepers."

"What? What did they share?" the doctor asked, laughing and frowning.

"Their beds. They spent the night with lepers."

Ilka began to groan softly and closed her eyes. "Here he goes again!" she mumbled.

"They spent the night with lepers?" the doctor smiled. "So you go spend the night with them, if you like. Go sleep with them, my friend. No one will disturb you. If the lepers don't protest, that is. But don't force others to do it, don't compel them. You don't have any right. No doubt I fail to understand these lofty topics very well, and it's quite likely that you'll develop into a splendid saint, but that you've developed into a bad husband, there is no longer the slightest doubt."

Fearfully, feebly Ilka shifted her eyes from the doctor to her husband. It seemed she was waiting for something, for a certain

The Fairy Karabos

moment, in order to rejoice. She was waiting yet dared not hope for that moment, she was so afraid.

Stanya began to swing his knee. "From what do you deduce, doctor, sir, that I'm a bad husband? Not from my concern about the child, I hope?"

"From what do I deduce? From the way you treat your wife. She is weak and nervous and requires exceptional attention and care at the present time, but instead you hurt her."

"I hurt her?" Stanya was sincerely surprised.

"Yes, you hurt her! Look, she doesn't want this witch, this Kazimira Karlovna, but you're pressuring her into it. And incidentally, don't imagine that it's modesty that makes Kazimira Karlovna not want to show herself in the park or to your guests. It's not because she considers herself deformed—not at all! It's simply distasteful to her that she has to become a domestic. She's actually a very arrogant lady. She curls her hair on curling papers and doesn't consider herself ugly at all. She repels the druggist, so he's damned glad to send her packing. No," he bent over and kissed Ilka's hand, "this scoffing at my dear patient we can't allow. It's simply not allowed, dear Stanislav Adamich. You'll have to find yourself other gates to Paradise."

He jumped up, silently pressed Ilka's and Stanya's hands, and quickly left the room. Through the window Ilka could see him turn onto the road toward the gates.

He was of average height and very thin.

Later, after many years, she would remember him as quite tall, broad-shouldered, and very much in love with her. Throughout her life she loved only him. But they didn't manage to, they did not know how to, they could not express their love to each other.

And sometimes, in rare dreams, he would come to her brightly and tenderly, and they would laugh and cry together. She would never remember his name.

Insurance

The restaurant was decorated in the old style, without checkered tablecloths on the tables or regional foods on the menu. Nevertheless, it was always crowded at lunchtime, with people clamoring for seats on the narrow, slippery banquettes.

The hors d'oeuvres had already been served, and no doubt there would now be an interminable wait for this idiotic "mixed grill." Why the boring Berestov had ordered a mixed grill instead of the roast duck everyone else was eating with great gusto, Dusya couldn't comprehend. Yes, everyone else gets to eat, but you have to sit and wait in order to please Mr. Berestov, who is in love with you and is therefore trying to outdo himself. You're sick of all this. You want to eat, not watch the others eating or see how moved Berestov is.

With her fork Dusya Brok angrily played with the sausage skins and shrimp shells on her plate, like a dog who has gobbled a tidbit thrown him by his master and now sniffs around the empty spot, pretending to be looking for something, thereby indicating to his master his craving for more.

Dusya Brok's pink and snub-nosed face, made up to appear healthy and gay, had grown unattractive from its expression of irritation and disappointment.

"Darling!" asked Berestov. "Why are you so sad?"

He drew her hand towards him to kiss it, but the angry Dusya purposely did not let go of her fork with the sausage skin dangling from it. So he let go of that hand and bending over, grasped the other, drawing it towards him to give it a smacking kiss. But just before smacking, he stopped short.

"Why aren't you wearing the perfume, the *Vortov*, I sent you?"

"I don't like *Vortov*. It smells like incense. I prefer my own, the Guerlain."

"Oh my God!" Berestov worried aloud. "I asked you to wear the *Vortov*. Was that so much to ask? Katyusha knows your perfume. Remember? The last time you and I were together at the theater, I come home, she sniffs around me and says: 'Who were you with? Why do you smell like Guerlain?' I say: 'Darling. That's *your* perfume.' And she answers: 'You're lying, I wear *Vortov*, and I'll find you out yet!' That's why I sent you the *Vortov*. And you don't want to wear it! Ai-ai-ai!"

"This is all wonderfully interesting and clever," Dusya muttered. "I'm supposed to pour some sort of stinking mess all over myself so that your family doesn't suffer. Why don't you just make your silly wife use a decent perfume? What if she takes it into her head to rub herself with garlic—then will all your ladies have to do the same?"

Berestov flushed and raised his red eyebrows.

"Dusya! Baby! Don't get angry. It's not becoming. Katyusha is convinced that when Dusya smiles, she grows fifty percent younger."

"And when Katyusha talks, she grows a full one hundred percent uglier. But let's drop this subject. You'd better tell me—do they intend to feed us today or should I abandon all hope? I can't sit here till evening simply because you had the unfortunate idea of ordering some kind of garbage that no one else is eating."

"Ha-ha! The cook here obviously doesn't hurry. As my wife says, he subscribes to the motto, 'More haste, less taste.' "

Berestov fell silent because suddenly he saw before him a monster. On the monster was Dusya's hat and Dusya's hair—oily yellow curls, two over each ear. You couldn't fail to recognize them. But the nose wasn't Dusya's. It had turned as white as chalk, and the nostrils flared. Under the nose throbbed the two red leeches of Dusya's mouth, the corners turned sharply down, and over the nose on either side stared two round grey buttons knotted in the center. And all of this quivered and gasped.

"Good Lord!" exclaimed Berestov. "Dusenka! What the hell is the matter with you?"

"What's wrong with me?" Dusya asked hoarsely. "What's wrong with me is that this has already gone too far. There are limits, you know. We haven't been sitting here more than a quarter of an hour and in that short time you've forced me to hear about your charming wife at least eight times. What she did, what she thought, even 'More haste, less taste.' Do you really think she made that up herself? It's an old, worn-out Russian proverb, it's the kind of folk nonsense everyone knows and repeats, but for some reason I'm supposed to get excited because your wife uttered it. There's one thing I don't understand, though: if you like her jokes and her anecdotes so much, why don't you eat lunch at home? Why do you hold a knife at my throat to get me to go out with you? I don't want to! I'm not interested! You always choose the kind of restaurant where no one goes—obviously, so you won't see anyone you know. We sit and wait for hours for some kind of grilled nonsense—don't interrupt me—nonsense of your own wild fancy, which we'll get sick from yet, and in the bargain, if you please, I have to listen to anecdotes from the life of your great wife. Is that what you take me out for? Don't dare interrupt me while I'm talking! . . . . However, I have nothing left to say."

Insurance

Dusya swallowed some wine, leaned back in her chair and suddenly said very simply and sadly: "You understand, you poor fool, that I was once ready to love you. But you spoiled everything."

"Dusya, darling," Berestov began uneasily. "Darling..." He obviously didn't know what to say.

Just then, after removing the decanters and plates, the waiter placed on the table a large platter laden with rosy pieces of grilled meats, sausages, mushrooms and kidneys, effectively skewered on tiny silver swords and sprinkled with fine straws of fried potatoes.

"Dusya!" Berestov said, wisely having waited for the first bites to pacify her. "I can explain everything, Dusya."

Just what he was going to say, he himself did not know. He didn't realize that the reason he talked about his wife all the time was because he wasn't supposed to. And because talking about her was so enjoyable, he almost felt as if he included her in their merry company and wasn't quite the bastard he was—one who often claimed he'd been to church, grabbed a bite to eat along the way and leisurely ambled home. Berestov had to disassociate himself from the bastard he was, if only by the fact that such a bastard would not dare talk about his wife, while Berestov actually enjoyed it.

Anyway, it was all so complicated that he himself couldn't understand it, so what was the point in explaining it to this marvellous quieted-down monster chewing crisp potato straws with her raspberry-red painted mouth? Berestov himself did not feel like eating. Large and heavy, he watched with raised eyebrows. When he saw his dear monster swallow, he swallowed too with his own empty mouth. He had to say *something*.

"Darling! I'll tell you the whole truth. Of course, I am very attached to my wife—to Katerina Nikolaevna, that is..."

"Not again!" Dusya groaned.

"No, no, I'm just explaining. We've been married twelve years. It's no longer attraction or passion, it's well-tried, solid friendship. I'm fifty years old, my dear child. She's over forty. I have gout. Excuse me for speaking about such dreary subjects, but I can't help it—they just come to mind. For me, as they say, it's time for winter quarters.* Katya is a kind woman, selflessly devoted, energetic, strong, healthy. I'd be lost without her help. She is, so to speak, wise insurance against the difficult, lonely sufferings which are already awaiting me somewhere beyond the door. You, Dusya, are my holiday, my secret quaff of champagne, necessary to my foolish male heart to keep it from suffering. And anyway, why deceive myself—I'm not necessary to you. You are a dancer, you have art and

---

*Here Berestov distorts a line from Mikhail Lermontov's poem "Borodino" (1837). (Trans.)

flirtations and joys, you still have a tremendous life ahead of you. But Katya... she's like a bone buried by an old dog for a rainy day. When the rainy day comes, the dog will dig it up."

"If it doesn't go rotten by then, that dog's bone of yours," Dusya muttered. And taking out a mirror, she began to powder her nose.

****

"Hello! Who's speaking?"

An unfamiliar voice replied. "This is Alexander Ilich Berestov's sister. He's sick and has instructed me to ask you to visit him. When could you come?"

"Oh, the poor thing! Has he been sick long? What's wrong with him?" Dusya asked in a shrill voice.

"A bad attack of gout. He's been sick a long time, about two weeks already. Will you come?"

"Of course I will! Oh, the poor thing, I didn't even know! Why didn't he tell me? I'll be over right away."

Within half an hour Dusya rang at the Berestovs' door. Since their unfortunate lunch—already over a month ago—she had not seen him at all. He had dropped by twice but hadn't caught her at home, so he had stopped coming. Then he had fallen ill. Dusya reasoned: now his "insurance" must be on the scene. But strictly speaking, she had nothing to feel uneasy about.

A Russian maid opened the door. "Please come in, he's expecting you. His sister just left."

"Is the lady of the house at home? Katerina Nikolaevna?"

"No, but the lady will probably be home for dinner. Right this way, please, he's in the bedroom."

The first thing Dusya saw was a pillow with something huge, round and bandaged on it.

"Good Lord! His head!" She was frightened.

But it wasn't his head—it was his foot—because at the other end of the bed, on another pillow, raised up, smiling and wincing, lay a yellow, swollen and poorly shaven face. It smiled, winced, then eased itself back onto the pillow.

"Come around here, dear. Thank you for coming. Forgive me for asking for you, it's just that I'm so terribly bored. My sister Vera, the kind soul, comes sometimes to amuse me. You can't imagine how the pain tires me though... At times it really tears at me, like pincers. I've been in bed two weeks now. It's dreadful."

"But where is Katerina Nikolaevna?"

Insurance

"Now you sit down, dear. Why are you standing? Katya is fine, thank you. Sit down here, so I can see you better. Yes, about the pain. During the day it's still tolerable, but at night I just don't know what to do. The nights are so long, they drag on and on. You turn out the light, then you turn it on, then off again, then on. Of course, hot poultices would help, but where can you get them at night? And then the loneliness begins to torment you! You don't want to show yourself to outsiders in such a state. I don't know how I ever got up my courage to ask for you."

"But what about Katerina Nikolaevna? Where is she?"

"Katya? Katya always has loads of things to do during the day, either her shopping or her drawing lessons . . . for some reason she suddenly fell in love with painting. My wife is lively and energetic. She runs around all day long and barely makes it home in time for dinner."

"Well, but—why can't she give you those poultices at night then? Things like that?"

The swollen face half laughed, half winced. "Come now, darling, you're talking like a child. My wife runs around all day—she has to sleep at night. My wife is strong and healthy. She needs her sleep, and here I am turning the light on and off twenty times a night. So of course she spends the nights at her brother's in Saint Cloud."

Dusya's voice began to quaver and it broke. "She spends the nights in Saint Cloud? Why in Saint Cloud?"

"She needs air, and I'm afraid of drafts. Besides, I make the whole apartment stuffy with the smell of grease. She's a healthy wife, she's strong, she needs air and a good night's rest. So while I'm sick, she absolutely cannot be staying here."

He looked intently at Dusya's face—which seemed to grow suddenly thin—at her unusually calm eyes, at her mouth opened in surprise.

"Yes, dear," he sighed. "Life is not a novel. Life demands clever calculations and a wise sensibility. Otherwise we'd all be up to no good! It's just lucky I have a sober mind. That's my insurance. But why are you so quiet, dear?"

Two Diaries

How interesting people's documents can be! I'm not talking about identity cards or passports or visas, though. What I have in mind are documents which bear witness to a man's secret, inner life, documents like a diary, kept for oneself alone and carefully hidden away from others' peering eyes.

Letters can never give reliable evidence about human personality, because they're written for a definite purpose or goal. One has to, let's say, appeal to a benefactor, or put a moocher in his place, or express sympathy, always heartfelt. Like congratulations, all of these occasions call for exaggerated tones. And then there are the refined letters, the literary ones, the flirtatious letters—what kinds aren't there! And they're all calculated for effect.

A secret diary is another matter. Here, almost everything is truthful and sincere. It's not intended for circulation—just the opposite—circulation is what we fear the most. Can we possibly consider Tolstoy's diaries trustworthy documents when we know what Sofia Andreevna asked him to downplay and delete?

A secret diary rarely falls into strange hands. I was just lucky. I was so lucky it's hard to believe: in my hands I have not one diary, but two. They belong to the Kashenevs, Pyotr Evdokimych and Marya Nikolaevna, who both kept diaries during the very same period of time, probably the most vivid period of their married life. And now, when you compare their entries day by day, you get such a vivid picture that you just want to scream: "The devil take it, you silly fool, where are your eyes?" You want to scream a lot more besides, but there's little sense in such belated exclamations. So you don't.

I now offer up to the reader's attention both diaries, selected according to dates. I'm not quoting all of the entries, of course. I've taken the liberty of omitting: "September 5. I bought a white collar on sale for 30 francs in Maison de Blanc. It turned out to be a bad buy—the collar is big enough for a cow."

That's from Marya Nikolaevna's diary. And from Pyotr Evdokimych's: "October 2. I got another blister on my crooked toe."

There are many entries of this ilk, ones which do not constitute a link in the general chain and which I deliberately omit.

Well then:

From the diary of Marya Nikolaevna Kasheneva:

November 1.

I don't think I'll ever forget last night! And no one who saw me will forget it either. I've never been so pretty and so lively! My eyes sparkled like diamonds. I was wearing a green dress which set off the marble of my shoulders and the alabaster of my back. My husband, that hypocrite, was angry, of course. He was jealous that he couldn't reveal his shoulders, too. Wouldn't that have been a sight!

Sergei couldn't take his mad eyes off me. But I flirted with that idiot Gozhkin to divert the hypocrite's suspicion. I was amazingly pretty, like a Bacchante. I ran up to the piano and sang, "I love you and long for your caresses." I sang marvellously. The best evidence was that Petrova and Kuzhina left in a huff, while my hypocrite squinted his furious eyes at me. Sergei Zapakin was pale as a sheet.

Petrova and Kuzhina were angry, I suppose. Poor dears, it's hard to compete with me. And besides, Kuzhina had stuffed herself into a turquoise caftan. What a fool!

The hypocrite made a scene, of course. But I just laughed.

From the diary of Pyotr Evdokimych Kashenev:

November 1.

A scandal to end all scandals! My fool of a wife suddenly began to sing! It was such a disgrace I'll be embarrassed to remember it as long as I live. Married seventeen years and never thought she had such an awful voice! And on top of that she accompanied herself obscenely out of tune. I was so ashamed I didn't know what to do, where to cast my eyes. That dear boy, Sergei Zapakin, suffered terribly for me. But Gozhkin (obviously all this was done for his benefit!) "thanked her for the pleasure afforded" in the most impudent way.

What a horror it was!

Petrova and Kuzhina—females of God knows what reputation —even they couldn't stand it. They jumped and fled.

We've lived together seventeen years, we've often had to deal with every kind of calamity, but that she'd begin to sing in our eighteenth year—that I could not foresee. Could not foresee at all. It simply boggles my mind.

After the guests left, we had a disgraceful scene. She laughed insolently. I, as the sufferer, shouted. I even broke the milk jar.

From Marya Nikolaevna's diary:

November 6.

Tomorrow is my birthday. I told Sergei about it. We *must* be together on such a joyful day!

For some reason Sergei fell to thinking. I invited Gozhkin for tomorrow, too, so that the hypocrite won't begin to suspect anything.

From Pyotr Evdokymich's diary:

November 6.

What good people there still are in the world! Yesterday Sergei Zapakin was very preoccupied for some reason. I asked him about it, and then the poor boy, with tears in his eyes, confessed that he has an old mother living in Belgium and he supports her as best he can. Right now he needs to send her 200 francs, but he doesn't have such a sum at his disposal and he's tormented terribly by it. Of course, I immediately offered the small sum. It was touching to see his gratitude.

From Marya Nikolaevna's diary:

November 8.

Sergei called yesterday morning. "I wanted to be the first to congratulate you. Please forgive my modest gift. I sent you some chrysanthemums."

Within an hour a huge basket of marvellous golden chrysanthemums was delivered to me. A basket like that must have cost 200 francs!

The hypocrite goes and gropes all around the basket, searching for the card. Then he says: "No matter, I know this is from Gozhkin. Your wiles won't save him. I'll kick his right down the stairs today."

From Pyotr Evdokymich's diary:

November 8.

Composure, composure, composure. I'll track down Gozhkin and finish him off.

From Marya Nikolaevna's diary:

November 20.

I said to Sergei: "This duplicity has exhausted me. I want to be with you, in your embraces, inseparably, for all my life, for all eternity."

"Eternity?" he repeated. "Why are you so depressed? Let's go to Saint Germain for a couple of days. Think something up."

I told the hypocrite that Liza Khryabina had invited me to visit her in Saint Cloud. She doesn't have a telephone, so it's impossible to check up on me, and there's no chance he'll pop up there, since he really can't stand Liza.

From Pyotr Evdokymich's diary:

November 20.
Sergei Zapakin was here today. He came to sit in my study. He was very preoccupied again. I immediately understood what was wrong. "What," I say, "your dear old mother is giving you trouble again?" He blushed a little. "Why," he says, "do you . . ." But I brought him to reason. "Why hide that from me?" He had no idea what to answer, so I put it to him frankly: "You probably need money for your mother?" Sergei was so touched by my shrewdness, he even began to laugh. I loaned him 400. Such a man is rare in our times.

November 21.
My fool wife has expressed the desire to go visit another fool in Saint Cloud. Can't you just see it: they go crazy when they don't see each other, their nerves run wild. We know these nerves. I said to her in the most innocent voice: "Go, my dear, and I'll ask Andrei Ivanich Gozhkin to come breakfast and dine with me, otherwise I'll be lonely all alone." In answer to that she burst into the most unnatural laughter. And it was the laughter that gave her away. She wanted to hide her vexation, but instead she only emphasized it by the unnaturalness of her behavior. Now let her sit in Saint Cloud. I'm certainly not going to rush her. In fact I might advise her to stay a little longer. Ha-ha!

From Marya Nikolaevna's diary:

February 2.
How strangely my hypocrite is acting! He has some kind of sick love for Gozhkin. He literally is never separated from him. I hardly even catch sight of Gozhkin when he comes to visit before my husband drags him into his study either to smoke or to play chess. On the other hand, he tries in every way to keep Sergei in my presence. He asks him to accompany me to the theater, the movies, even visiting. All of this is very strange. Maybe he's thinking of catching us by surprise? Not long ago he went to Rouen for two days

and took Gozhkin with him. "You've never been there," he said. "You're a young man, you have to develop." And he took him along. This is becoming downright indecent! Naturally, Gozhkin is glad for the free ride.

From Pyotr Evdokymich's diary:

February 2.
Sergei Zapakin is a dear fellow, but I'm finding that his old lady is a bit of a bore. I'm beginning to get tired of her. Either she has to get something for a holiday, or she needs a winter coat, or she has to go to the doctor. And somehow it's already become commonplace that I help out... But still, from his point of view, it's touching. That dried-up Gozhkin probably doesn't even think about old women. And Sergei Zapakin thinks about nothing but his dear old mother! A rare young man.

From Marya Nikolaevna's diary:

June 20. Vichy.
I really don't know how to explain this. Sergei doesn't answer my letters. He promised to come, but he's still not here. My hypocrite has become totally unhinged. In the spring he went with his Gozhkin to Corsica, now he's sitting with him in Paris, and *he* doesn't answer my letters either. I'm really going out of my mind. But what's the matter with Sergei?

From Pyotr Evdokymich's diary:

June 25.
How repulsive this idiot Gozhkin's face has become to me! Every day he dines with me and stays all evening. But it's impossible to let him go—he'll make for Vichy straight away. He's gotten fat as a hog on free food, and he snores in my armchair. He's flooded with lard. What did she ever see in him?

June 26.
An event. Zapakin came over, terribly upset. It turns out that his old mother has to have an operation, and right away. As he talked, tears flooded his eyes and his lips quivered. "This," he says, "is the last time I'll come running for your help. In two weeks I'm going to marry a very wealthy lady, but it's still a secret." Well, I congratulated him and gave him money for the operation. "Write," I said, "and tell me how she bears up and whether she suffers a lot." He promised to.

All About Love

From Marya Nikolaevna's diary:

June 28.
My God, what I've lived through! Yesterday Sergei finally came. It's all over. He's getting married.

From Pyotr Evdokymich's diary:

July 1.
I received a telegram from my Seriozhka Zapakin. "She bore up well, didn't suffer badly, died forever." A strange telegram. I wonder whether I'll have to send money for the funeral.

July 2.
Aha! A telegram from my dear wife (!): "In a terrible state, if you yourself can't come, send Gozhkin."

Aha! Just as I thought! She finally cried out, the low-down woman. Let her have Gozhkin! Now she and I are going to have our talk. I'm leaving on the evening train.

The Nightmare

The nightmare lasted four years.

Four years poor Vera Sergeevna knew no peace day or night. Day and night she was conscious of the fact that her happiness was dangling on a thread, that today or tomorrow that insolent hussy, Eliza Gertz, might steal Nikolai Andreevich away from her once and for all. He was already enamoured of her.

Poor Vera Sergeevna fought for her heart and hearth with every resource that modern civilization had placed in the hands of a sensible and energetic woman: she wrote herself anonymous letters and then showed them to her wayward husband; she assured him constantly of their son's brilliant intellect and emphasized how important firm family foundations were for the nurturance of such a chosen creature; she created a comfortable and cozy domestic life and planned interesting parties, to which she invited prominent people; she took care of her appearance, exercised, was massaged, painstakingly performed her toilette, did everything she could to be young, intelligent, and beautiful in the eyes of her husband. Never, even in the first years of their married life, had she been so in love with him, as in these four years of the nightmare.

And indeed, if Nikolai Andreevich could have been attractive to anyone, it would have been during these four years. He had become elegant, vigorous, and mysterious, now stormily cheerful, now melancholy. He recited verse and gave his wife presents, even compliments—mainly, we suppose, as he was hurrying out of the house, afraid of being detained.

"Darling, how attractive you are today," he would mutter distractedly, kissing her forehead. "You should always wear that dress."

Or: "Are you having guests today? I'm terribly sorry I can't be here. But I'll send you a basket of flowers. Let everyone see that I'm still in love with my kitten."

He always smelled of stirring scents, although he himself didn't use any. He was always humming something, exuding an air of infatuation—at which everyone would smile uneasily, casting sly glances at each other and tittering themes of love.

Once a year Eliza Gertz gave a concert. Vera Sergeevna would order a magnificent toilette for that evening. She'd gather her friends together at dinner and then invite them to her loge. Nikolai Andreevich would sit separately in the parterre, and she would follow the expression of his face with her opera glasses.

All About Love

Nikolai Andreevich really was enchanted with Eliza Gertz. His quiet, careful, businesslike nature was as unlike Eliza's personality as the land from the sea, yet he swam in her, dove, and snorted with pleasure. All her elegant rabble amazed and moved him: the polished dandies with stomachs rumbling with hunger; the languishing ladies with glued-on eyelashes, whose belongings were always being held by some hotel for non-payment of their rooms; the breakfasts at five in the evening, dinners at one in the morning, unexpected dances—all the intricacies of the relationships between these strange and fascinating people. And the strangest and most fascinating of all—incomprehensible, unknown to the end, tormenting both herself and others, brilliant, talented, goddess, devil, snake—was Eliza Gertz.

In all four years Nikolai Andreevich was not for a single day calm or sure of what the next day would bring. He never understood a thing about her.

One day she returned the expensive bracelet he had sent her, scrawling in pencil on a scrap of paper: "I didn't expect such boorishness. I'm embarrassed for you." Confused and humiliated, he did not dare appear before her for two whole days and wracked his brains to understand why she could have taken such offense when just three days earlier he had given her twenty thousand which she nonchalantly dropped into her purse, actually yawning in the process.

Another time, after receiving a basket of oranges from him, she got down on her knees before him and said there was so much innocent beauty in this action of his that she had cried tears of ecstasy all morning, then ordered a compote made from the oranges.

He never knew what was awaiting him. He often returned home offended and humiliated and sought consolation in Vera Sergeevna's devotion.

"Verusya, you're an angel, and I'm a pig," he would say. "But you know even a pig has a right to demand his share of respect and affection. Hug me, tell me, is our Volodya really a remarkable boy? I want to live for you and for him only. Really, just for the two of you!"

Sometimes, like a meteor, like a meteor sparkling with joy, he would run home for just a moment, humming an operetta tune: "Good-bye, Verusya. You are my life. Don't hold me back—some boring business is calling. Tra-la-la! Boring, tra-la-la! Business, la-de-da!"

And off he'd go again.

****

The Nightmare

The nightmare ended unexpectedly.

For a long time Eliza had been talking about a singing engagement in Argentina. Nikolai Andreevich had grown used to these discussions and didn't pay any particular attention to them. From time to time he had to sign checks made out to some middleman, but then he often had to give out money for the most incomprehensible needs—for some sort of advertising (what sort he didn't know), for liquidating a debt from a concert that was absolutely assured to bring in a profit, and so on. Consequently he didn't give special significance to these middlemen. Then suddenly it turned out that the Argentinian tour was not a mirage at all, but an imminent reality, and Eliza had only to secure a passport to leave right away.

The proposed half-year's separation didn't particularly bother Nikolai Andreevich, though, at least not at first. "I'll relax, have a long sleep, and conduct my business affairs," he cheered himself.

Eliza's whole set went to see her off in Marseilles. It was an intoxicating, merry occasion.

For a long time Nikolai Andreevich could not tear himself away from Eliza's life. He made the rounds of restaurants with her friend Milusha in order to talk about Eliza, try to learn more about her and verify certain facts he already had.

Then he got tired of Milusha. She was dumb and unattractive and wore Eliza's old dresses. And everything she said about her friend somehow simplified Eliza, made her comprehensible, deprived her of anxieties and mysteries.

He soon got rid of Milusha.

Then a letter came from Eliza with tales of raging success and a request for money.

With great delight he immediately sent the sum demanded.

Five months later a second demand arrived.

He fulfilled that, too, but no longer with delight.

Her letters smelled of a new perfume, like incense. Very disagreeable.

Nikolai Andreevich became bored. Weariness from the sleepless nights, the drinking binges, and the anxieties of the past year soon told on him. He took to lazily dealing out solitaire, grumbling at his wife, and falling into bed at ten o'clock.

At first Vera Sergeevna regarded the happy change in her life with pleasure. Then she began to worry because her flighty husband, who had always given her complete freedom, suddenly sat immobile at home. Twice he expressed great indignation when she returned home late from her bridge game. She felt some annoyance and even boredom from such behavior on his part.

"Well, this shouldn't last long," she consoled herself. "That woman will return soon enough and everything will be as it was before."

But everything wasn't as it was before.

Nikolai Andreevich received a new demand from Argentina, which he venomously answered by telegram: "You will receive it only if we meet in person." The answer came over the wire, a single word in roman letters: "Bastard."

Vera Sergeevna, who by rights of an innocent sufferer often rummaged through her unfaithful husband's desk (she had even equipped herself very cleverly with a small button hook for this purpose), read this telegram with mixed emotions of despair and delight.

Delight sang: the nightmare is over.

Despair moaned: what will happen now?

And despair was right.

The once fascinating and tender Nikolai Andreevich, now like a dishevelled boar, leapt out of his study with bills in his hands and gave his poor suffering wife such a chewing out for the dress from Chanel and the hat from Desca, that she bitterly longed for the difficult years of the nightmare.

And then a new misfortune appeared: their "brilliant" boy turned out to be dumb. He had failed to get his diploma for the third time, and when his father—with reason—called him an idiot, the young scion, sticking his upper lip out like a trunk, said very clearly: "Idiot? It must be hereditary."

Suddenly the parents noticed with horror that he was lop-eared, with a low forehead and a dirty neck. In general, he was nothing to be proud of. But it was already too late to thrash him. Vera Sergeevna reproached her husband for neglecting the child, and her husband reproached her for fussing over him too much. Everything was unpleasant and dull.

In such an atmosphere it was no use even thinking about maintaining their former way of life. What need was there for parties with refined guests? And on top of everything else, Nikolai Andreevich was becoming carping and stingy. He hung around the house, eternally sticking his nose into everything. It got to the point that when Vera Sergeevna bought a piece of smoked sturgeon for dinner, he called her, in front of the servant, a witch, always choosing a word inappropriate to the given occasion, but one which was nonetheless very insulting and coarse.

So that's how things were.

Nikolai Andreevich tried to rouse himself. He took a young ballerina out to dinner. But he was so bored with her that later, when

The Nightmare

she began to call him every day on the telephone, he asked his wife, Vera Sergeevna, to put the ballerina in her place for him.

Vera Sergeevna stopped dressing up and taking care of herself. She unravelled at the seams and aged quickly.

She often fell to thinking bitterly: "Yes! Not too long ago I was a woman who lived a full life. I loved, envied, and sought oblivion in the whirl of society."

"How boring Paris has become," she would sigh. "Not at all the same atmosphere. Everything is somehow extinguished and gloomy."

"It's all on account of the recession," friends explained to her.

She would shake her head mistrustfully, and one time, turning pale and flushing, she asked the old profligate, Colonel Eroshin, her husband's friend: "Tell me, do you know why that singer, Eliza Gertz, doesn't return from South America?"

"God knows," the Colonel answered indifferently. "Maybe she doesn't have the money to come back."

"Don't you think it would be worth it to send her money for the trip?" Vera Sergeevna asked, even more agitated. "Maybe you could talk it over with my husband? Hm?"

About Eternal Love

It rained this afternoon. Now the garden is damp.

We're sitting on the terrace watching the little lights of Saint Germain and Viroflay flicker on the distant horizon. From here, from our high forested hill, this distance seems like an ocean: we can make out the lanterns on the pier, the flashes from the lighthouse, the signal lights of ships. Total illusion.

It's quiet.

Through the open doors of the salon we hear the last melancholy, passionate strains of "The Dying Swan," which the radio brings us from some distant land. Then it's quiet once again.

We sit in the twilight. The ember of a cigar blazes up and rises like a small red eye.

"Why are we so silent, like a Rockefeller digesting his dinner? After all, we haven't set ourselves the goal of living to be a hundred," a baritone voice speaks out in the twilight.

"Is Rockefeller silent?"

"He's quiet for half an hour after breakfast and half an hour after dinner. He started keeping quiet at the age of forty. Now he's ninety-three. And he always invites guests to dinner."

"What about them?"

"They stay quiet, too."

"What foolishness!"

"Why do they do it?"

"Because they hope. If a poor man took it into his head to stay silent while digesting his food, no one would go see the old fool. But a Rockefeller... No doubt he feeds his guests some sort of hygienic carrots?"

"Of course! And to top it off, he chews each piece of food no less than sixty times."

"What an imbecile!"

"Let's talk about something more appetizing. Petrony, tell us about one of your adventures."

The cigar blazed up, and Petrony (so called because his gaiters and neckties matched his suit) said in a lazy voice: "Well, why not, if you want me to. What about?"

"Something about eternal love," a woman's voice said clearly. "Have you ever encountered eternal love?"

"Of course! All the love I've ever encountered has been eternal. Without exception."

"Are you kidding? Really? Tell us about just one case."

"One case... There are so many that it's hard to choose."

"And they're all of them eternal?"

"All are eternal. Well, now, I could tell you about a little train-car adventure... It happened long ago, of course. It's not polite to talk about the recent ones. This was in prehistoric times, that is, before the war. I was travelling from Kharkov to Moscow. As you know, the trip is long and boring, but I'm a good man—fate took pity on me and at a small station sent me a most attractive travelling companion. I looked at her—she's stern, doesn't look at me, reads a book, nibbles on candy. Still, in the end we started talking. The lady turned out to be sterner than I'd imagined. From almost her first sentence she announced that she loves her husband with an eternal love, to the grave, amen.

"Well, what the hell, I think, that's a good sign. Imagine that you meet a tiger in the jungle. You freeze and feel unsure of your hunting skills and your strength. And suddenly the tiger sticks his tail between his legs, crawls behind a bush and rolls up his eyes. That means he's frightened. It's obvious. So this love to the grave was just the bush behind which my lady hid herself.

"Well, once she takes fright, you have to tread softly.

"'Yes, ma'am,' I say, 'I believe you and bow down to you. What do we live for, tell me, if we can't believe in eternal love? What a horror inconstancy is! Today a little affair with one, tomorrow with another—it's just plain disagreeable, not to mention immoral. So much trouble, such intrigue. You get someone's name mixed up—and you know how sensitive they are, these love objects. You accidentally call Manichka Sonichka, and such complications begin that you'll wish you were dead! As if the name Sofia is any worse than Maria! Or else you mix up an address and thank some fool you haven't seen for two months for the raptures of her love, while the new little one gets a letter in which you speak in a severe tone about the fact that, unfortunately, you can't get back what's past. In general, all of this is dreadful, although I, of course, only know about such things by hearsay, since I myself am capable only of eternal love—except this eternal love hasn't turned up for me yet.'

"My lady listened; she even opened her mouth. Quite a charming lady. She was completely tamed. She even began to say you and I. 'You and I understand, you and I believe.'

"I, of course, said you and I, too, but always in the most respectful tones, with eyes lowered and quiet tenderness in my voice. I used ploy number six on her.

"By twelve o'clock I had already progressed to number eight and suggested that we have lunch together.

About Eternal Love

"We became great friends over lunch. Although there was one problem—she still talked a whole lot about her husband. Everything was 'my Kolya, my Kolya,' and there was no way you could get her off the topic. I, of course, kept hinting that he wasn't worthy of her, but I didn't dare overdo it, since that always calls forth protests, and protests wouldn't have served the matter at hand.

"By the way, about that hand... I was already kissing her hand with complete freedom—as much as I wanted to and however I wanted to.

"Now the train is approaching Tula and suddenly it dawns on me: 'Listen, darling! Let's get off quickly and wait for the next train. I beg of you! Hurry!'

"She was confused. 'Whatever for?'

"'What do you mean, whatever for?' I cried in a rush of inspiration. 'We'll go to Tolstoy's grave. Yes, yes! It's the sacred responsibility of every cultured person. Porter!'

"She became even more confused. 'So you're saying ... cultured responsibility ... of a sacred person ...'

"But she herself dragged her cardboard box down from the shelf.

"We managed to jump off just as the train started up again.

"'What about Kolya? He's planning to meet me.'

"'To Kolya,' I say, 'we'll send a telegram saying you'll arrive on the night train.'

"'But what if he ...'

"'Is that really something we have to worry about? If anything, he should thank you for such a beautiful gesture. To visit the grave of a great old man in these days of general unbelief and disdain for societal pillars!'

"I seated my lady at the buffet and went to hire a cab. I asked the porter to hire a cabby a little more reckless than others—why not? It would make the drive more pleasant.

"The porter smirked. 'We understand,' he said. 'We can oblige you.'

"The rogue obliged me so much I could hardly believe it: a troika with bells, just as though it were carnival time!

"Well, why not, all the better.

"We set out. We passed Kozlova Zaseka, and I said to the cabby: 'Maybe it would be better to tie up your bells? It's awkward driving along with such ringing going on. After all, we're going to a grave, you know.'

"But he didn't pay any attention 'That doesn't matter to us,' he says. 'There's no one says you can't do it and no one says you can. Everyone drives the way he wants to.'

"We arrived at the grave, read the admirers' inscriptions on the fence: 'Tolya and Mura were here'; 'Sashka-Kanashka and Abrasha from Rostov were here!' 'I love Marya Sergeevna Abinosova, Evgeny Lukin.' 'M. D. and K. V. smashed Kuzma Vostrukhin in the kisser.' And there were various drawings: a heart pierced by an arrow; an ugly face with horns; initials. That's how the grave of the great writer was honored. We looked around, walked a bit and raced back in the troika.

"We still had a long time to wait for the train, and we couldn't just sit in the station. So we went to a restaurant. I asked for a private room: 'What point is there,' I say, 'in revealing ourselves? We might meet an acquaintance, some old-fashioned, vulgar boor who doesn't understand the cultural and spiritual needs of the soul.'

"We spent the time wonderfully. And when it was time to leave for the station, my little lady says: 'This pilgrimage made such an indelible impression on me that I'm going to repeat it without fail, and the sooner, the better.'

"'Darling!' I cried. 'Exactly—the sooner, the better. Let's stay here till tomorrow. We'll go to Yasnaya Polyana* in the morning and take the train from there.'

"'And my husband?'

"'Your husband will remain as such. Since you love him with an eternal love, what difference does it make? After all, it's an unshakeable feeling.'

"'Then, according to you, I don't have to tell Kolya anything?'

"'Kolya? It goes without saying we won't tell Kolya anything. Why worry him?'"

At this point the storyteller fell silent.

"Well, what happened then?" asked a female voice.

The storyteller sighed. "We went to Tolstoy's grave three days in a row. Then I went to the post office and sent myself an urgent telegram: 'Vladimir, come home immediately.' I signed it: 'Your wife.'"

"Did she believe it?"

"Yes. She got very angry. But I said: 'Darling, who can appreciate eternal love better than you and I? You see, my wife also loves me with an eternal love. We must respect her emotion.' And that's the end."

"It's time to go to bed, everyone," someone said.

"No, let's have another story. Madame G-ch, maybe you know one?"

---

*Yasnaya Polyana is the name of Tolstoy's estate near Tula. (Trans.)

About Eternal Love

"Me? About eternal love? Actually, I do know a little story, and it's very, very short. I once had a dove on my farm, and I asked my servant, a Pole, to bring a female from Poland for the male. He brought it. The female hatched some little nestlings and then she flew away. They caught her, but she flew away again. It was obvious she was languishing for her homeland. She left her mate for Poland."

"Tout comme chez nous," one of the listeners interjected.

"She gave up her mate and two babies. The male began to keep them warm himself. But it was cold, wintertime, and the male's wings are shorter than the female's. The babies froze. We took them away. And for ten days the male didn't eat his food, he weakened, he fell from his roost. In the morning we found him on the ground, dead. That's all."

"That's all? Then let's go to bed."

"Oh well," said someone, yawning. "A bird... is like an insect, that is, I mean to say, a lower animal. It can't reason. It lives instinctively. By some kind of reflexes. Scholars are studying them now, these reflexes, and soon they'll be able to heal everyone. There won't be any more amorous anguish, dying swans, or crazy doves. They'll all be like the Rockefellers! They'll chew sixty times, keep quiet and live to be a hundred. Won't that be splendid?"

The Suitor

In the evening after work, Bulbezov liked to keep himself busy.

His pursuits were of a particular kind: he wrote letters either to the editorial offices of a newspaper, or directly to the authors of articles which displeased him. He wrote threateningly:

"Dear Sir:
Yesterday I had the displeasure of reading your usual humbug. In your 'historical' essay you write: 'At Danton's words an electric current seemed to run through the crowd.'

I hasten to bring to your attention that at the time of the French Revolution, electricity had not yet been discovered, so there is no way an electric current could have run through the crowd. It would not hurt you to know this, since you have the audacity and conceit to take up a pen and lecture everyone.
Ilya B--."

Or else he wrote something like this:

"Dear Mr. Editor Sir:
Please direct your attention to the article by your science columnist. In issue number sixty-two of your respected newspaper this free-and-easy fellow, with characteristic brashness, discusses the mind of the ant. But where, in that case, is the ant's skull? I personally have never seen one, although I used to live in the country. All of this contradicts common sense.
A reader, but not an admirer,
Ilya B--."

He attacked not only contemporary writers, but classical ones, too.

"Dear Mr. Editor Sir:
Allow me by means of your respected newspaper to call the attention of public opinion to the writings of the illustrious Lev Tolstoy. In Part 2, Chapter 4, of his work *War and Peace*, the famous count writes: 'Alpatych, having arrived in Smolensk on the evening of August 4, stayed in the Gachensky suburbs beyond the Dnepr at the inn kept by the yardman Ferapontov, with whom he had customarily stayed for the past thirty years. Ferapontov, who with

Alpatych's help had bought a grove from the prince *thirty years ago* and started a trading business, now had a house, an inn, and a flour shop in the province. Ferapontov was a fat, dark, ruddy, *forty-year-old* muzhik, with thick lips, and so on.'

Please note: a forty-year-old muzhik bought a grove thirty years ago and began to trade. That means the muzhik was exactly ten years old at the time. I consider that a slander on the Russian people. And just because Count Tolstoy thought this up, why must everyone bow down to him, while if some peasant—no Count Lev T.—were to write like that, he would not be published?

It's not democratic.

    I.B."

Bulbezov rewrote these letters very carefully. He kept one copy for himself, numbered it, and hid it.

He took his pursuits very seriously and never allowed himself to waste the evening at a movie or a cafe, as all sorts of idlers do.

"So long as I have the strength to work, I'll work."

****

How it happened, no one knows.

Maybe Spring wafted strange thoughts to him?

Although it may well be that Spring had nothing to do with it at all. Because if it were Spring, then Bulbezov no doubt would have admired the blossoming trees, the young couples kissing under their boughs, the bouquets of first violets offered by the old women of Paris, their voices hoarse and thick with red wine. Or, he would have caught a glimpse of the moon, always a gratifying sight for lovers, if he'd only opened his window and leaned to the right. But Bulbezov did not open the window and did not lean out. Bulbezov had no time for the moon.

The whole thing began not with the moon and not with flowers, not with trifles in general. It began with a button torn off a vest and continued with a hole in the knee, that is, not in the knee itself, but in the clothing which covered it. To make a long story short, it all began with a pants leg.

And it all ended with a decision. But don't assume that it was a decision to sew or to darn. In that case, would there be a story to tell?

No, Bulbezov took it into his head to get married.

And as soon as he thought of it, the thought travelling along the thread from button to needle grabbed his hand, which was holding the needle, and jabbed him in the neck: why not marry Maria Sergeevna Utina?

The Suitor

"Why not marry Utina?

"She's young and pleasant. She works. She sews. Why, she'll sew everything, she'll darn everything I own."

Here Bulbezov felt surprise—why hadn't he thought of this before? After all, if he'd hit upon the idea sooner, then the button would now be sitting in place and he himself would now be sitting in place, and he would not have to drag himself over to Utina's to try to explain his feelings. Utina would be sitting here, too, following him with loving eyes as he worked.

****

It would be foolish to put it off.

He changed his collar and smoothed down his hair. Then, with obvious pleasure, he gazed at himself for a long time in the mirror, at his large, pock-marked nose, his sunken cheeks, his Adam's apple covered with goose bumps.

There was nothing surprising in his pleasure, however, since most men are pleased by what they see in the mirror. A woman is always worried about something, grumbling or fixing something. Either she needs long eyelashes, or why doesn't she have a button mouth, or now she absolutely must bleach her hair. She's always troubling over something. But a man simply glances at himself—turning just a bit for the profile—and he's ready. Satisfied. Doesn't dream about anything and doesn't fret.

But let's not get distracted.

After admiring himself and taking out a clean handkerchief, Bulbezov set off with a decisive step along Cambron Street towards Vaugirard.

Night fell.

The passersby, tired and preoccupied, jostled each other on the sidewalk.

A gendarme chased an old flower vendor from the street. The bell of a movie house pierced the air like a sharp gimlet.

Bulbezov turned after the banished flower vendor and bought a branch of mimosa.

"It's easier to get a conversation going with flowers."

The spiral staircase of the small hotel was filled with the edible smells of fish, cabbage and onion. Behind every door spoons tinkled and plates clattered.

"*Entrez!*" Maria Sergeevna's voice answered his knock.

When he entered she jumped up, quickly shoved a cup into the cupboard and wiped her mouth.

"Now don't be embarrassed, please, it seems I've disturbed you," Bulbezov began in a genteel tone, handing the mimosa to her. "Here!"

Maria Sergeevna took the flowers, blushed, and began to straighten her hair. She was plump, with fluffy curls and a pug nose—very pleasant.

"Oh, you shouldn't have brought these!" she mumbled in confusion, casting several surprised, sly glances at Bulbezov. "Sit down, please. Excuse me, everything here is a mess. Lots of work. Wait a minute, I'll turn on the light."

Bulbezov, who was just about to give her a compliment ("You know, you're so charming that I couldn't resist running over here"), suddenly pricked up his ears.

"How did you choose to express that? What did you say?"

"Me?" Maria Sergeevna was surprised. "I said I'll turn on the light now. What's wrong with that?"

And going over to the door, she turned on the switch for the overhead lamp. She turned it on and, flooded with light, coquettishly raised her head.

"Sorry," Bulbezov said drily. "I thought I misheard you, but you repeated the same absurdity again—intentionally, I can only assume."

"What?" Maria Sergeevna was confused.

"You said, 'I'll turn on the light.' How is it possible, I'd like to know, to turn on light? You can turn on a table lamp, you can turn on a reading lamp, and finally, you can turn on a floor lamp. Then there will be light. But how are you going to turn on light? Take a lit match over to a fire, hm? Ha-ha! No, I don't like it, this 'turn on the light'!"

"What are you nit-picking about?" Maria Sergeevna muttered, pouting. "Everyone says that and no one has ever acted surprised."

In indignation Bulbezov stood up to his full height and straightened his shoulders. And having straightened himself, he found his head level with the mirror over the washstand, which reflected his face blazing with indignation.

He stood still for a second, absorbed in this magnificent sight. He looked at himself facing the mirror, then gazed at his profile with squinting eyes. He felt a surge of inspiration and exclaimed:

"'Everyone says that'! How dreadful to hear such a sentence! Or do you think that everything all of you do is intelligent? How startling! How offensive even! You, whom I chose and singled out, you turn out to be closely allied to 'everyone'! Well, thanks a lot! Everything you're all doing is so very smart—buckling up your armor to go investigate the stratosphere, or using some crazy Dog Star measurements a hundred kilometers up in outer space. But

The Suitor

have you measured everything here on earth, on your own earth? Just what do you know about electricity? Like parrots you've learned by rote, 'Anode and cathode and down the middle a spark.' But do you even know what a cathode is?"

"Get away from me!" Maria Sergeevna screamed. "When did I ever bug you with a cathode? I don't know any and I don't want to."

"You and yours are all alike," Bulbezov roared. "You strive for the moon and for Mars. But have you studied the average current of the Amazon? Or Central Africa with its impenetrable jungles?"

"What are you giving me these jungles for? I've lived without jungles and I'll go on living without them," Maria Sergeevna shouted in return.

"Can you cure tuberculosis? Have you discovered the cancer bacillus?" Bulbezov raged, ignoring her. "What do you need the stratosphere for? You'll get nothing from your stratosphere, you pigs, you ignoramuses!"

"You boor! You troublemaker!" Maria Sergeevna shouted tremulously. "Get out of here! Out! Or I'll call for the concierge!"

"I'm going! And I'm sorry I ever came! Louse!"

Bulbezov mechanically grabbed the branch of mimosa that had been left on the table and, bending it in half, stuck it into the pocket of his overcoat.

"Louse!" he repeated, casting a quick glance at himself in the mirror. He felt to make sure the mimosa was in his pocket and then, for effect, turned his back on his hostess and left.

Maria Sergeevna stared after him for a long time, dumbfounded.

Mr. Furtenau's Cat

It all happened on the church square in the small town of Sonnebach.

Actually, Sonnebach was no longer a town; it had merged with a big city and become a suburb of sorts. But in spirit it remained a town as before—remote, quiet and poor.

Its inhabitants worked mainly for the rich townspeople who lived beyond the bridge. Washwomen carted laundered linens there; teachers living in Sonnebach's cheap apartments scurried to give lessons in the big city schools. Various petty employees—bureaucrats, shop assistants, doctors' aides—left Sonnebach by trolley each morning for the whole day.

The apartments in Sonnebach rarely came vacant, especially not the small ones. As a matter of fact, one old witch who'd sat in her room and knitted for almost forty years had barely been laid to rest when into her spotless and cozy two-room apartment with kitchen moved a new tenant.

The new tenant was a tall, thin old man, very serious and polite. He was followed by a workman pulling his belongings in a hand-drawn cart: a sofa covered with oilcloth, an armchair, a folding chair, and a large cage wrapped up in green rags.

The small boys of the town, gaping at this procession, immediately guessed that a cat had arrived in the cage. Their guess was confirmed that very evening when they heard the old man calling his cat and it meowing in return.

"Peetie! Peetie! Peetie!" he called. "Want some milk?"

And the cat replied: "Meow! Meow!"

It answered rather gruffly. It must have been a tomcat, and not a young one at that.

And so the old man settled into his new home.

Like all the others, he took the trolley into the city each morning, returning in the evening with paper cones full of food, to keep house and talk to his cat, who always answered, "Meow."

As usual, the neighbors were curious at first, and they asked the watchman's wife who the new tenant was, where he worked, and why no one came to visit him on holidays—after all, everyone has *someone* to visit him, either relatives or friends.

But the watchman's wife could tell them little. She was generally admitted into the apartment only once a week, on Saturdays, to scrub the kitchen floor and launder the old man's nonsense. He did not let her into his rooms, preferring to clean them

All About Love

himself. The old man was neat and clean, but not very talkative, it seemed.

"He's just like an old maid," the watchman's wife described him. "And he works in liquidation."

Just what this "liquidation" was, no one understood, but as long as the old man worked, so God be with him. If a man works, it means you can understand him. He's no thief or murderer, you won't have to give testimony against him. So the neighbors soon got used to the fact that he was the silent type. What did this old man, the loner, have to talk about anyway? Maybe his cat? But that's just the sort of thing that people who dislike animals hate hearing the most. And those who do like them, why they themselves want to talk about their own favorite creature: what a gentle kitten they have, or what a devoted dog, or what a quick-witted chicken. In short, no one lost a thing from the old man's silence.

His last name was Furtenau.

Day followed day, night followed night. The spring days were clear, the summer hot, winter cold, and autumn boring.

The wind blew. A rusty weathervane on the spire of the old belltower squeaked. The moon drifted. It was a dull routine.

The neighbors got used to the old man, but they didn't especially like his dear cat.

To begin with, they got tired of the incessant conversations: "Peetie! Peetie! Peetie! Want some milk? Meow! Meow!"

They simply got tired of them. They even began to wish he'd beat his cat—at least that might change its yowl.

Then something happened. A large piece of fried sausage disappeared from the kitchen of Mr. Furtenau's neighbor. This neighbor's kitchen was located right next to Mr. Furtenau's, and the neighbor's niece, who slept in the kitchen, heard a noise in her sleep as if someone were scraping at the open window. A small ledge led from Mr. Furtenau's window to the neighbor's window, so that a cat could easily slip through and steal sausage.

The neighbor grieved and grieved over the sausage and ordered her niece to close the window at night. But one time the niece forgot, and Mr. Furtenau's cat didn't let the opportunity pass him by. It sniffed to make sure the way was clear, then carried off a good-sized chunk of ham.

The neighbor was beside herself. She kept watch on the street all day for Mr. Furtenau, and when she spied him, she ran out to say: "Respected neighbor, you absolutely must close the window to your kitchen, because the cat has already stolen meat from me two times."

Mr. Furtenau's Cat

In answer to this Mr. Furtenau removed his hat and said: "Thank you, but I don't buy meat."

And he left.

" 'I don't buy meat.' He doesn't buy meat! That's exactly why his cat goes and steals from other people's kitchens. The old man's an utter fool."

The neighbors discussed this question for a long time.

Later a piece of smoked fish disappeared, but then the neighbor's niece got married, and her groom, guzzling champagne at the wedding, confessed that his bride had stolen all of it—the fried sausage, and the ham, and the smoked fish—and had secretly brought the booty to him out in the barn where he had been skulking night after night out of insuperable love for his bride.

"So that's why Mr. Furtenau thanked me when I told him the cat steals meat! He thought I was warning him about someone else's cat."

And so it came to pass that the neighbors stopped slandering Mr. Furtenau's cat and became more indulgent towards the old man's annoying cries, "Peetie! Peetie! Peetie!"

****

Mr. Furtenau's apartment was on the top floor. A young bookbinder lived below him. Once a week the small blue-eyed washwoman Marishka delivered his laundry.

Perhaps the bookbinder was not so young any more, but he still lived alone. Each time Marishka delivered his laundry, she would very lengthily count out four handkerchiefs, two towels, and a pillow case. These complicated sums were somehow hard for her to do. And whenever she left the apartment, she would sigh.

One day the bookbinder took her by the hand and said with joyful surprise: "Good heavens! What blue eyes you have, Marishka!"

She blushed and was tormented all night: What did it mean? Was it good or bad that her eyes were blue?

One day the bookbinder complained to her that he was tired of listening to the old man's conversations with his cat. Marishka smiled sadly and said: "But I feel so sorry for him! After all, he has no one in the whole world besides that cat. He comes home old and tired and calls to his cat. The cat answers 'meow' and goes up to him, alive and warm. He pets the cat and it rubs up against him. That's how they love each other, and their love protects them."

"Protects them from what?"

"I don't know. From fear . . . I don't know."

The bookbinder became thoughtful. Then he said: "Well, let the old man call 'Peetie! Peetie!' as much as he likes. I won't get angry any more."

A week later, when Marishka came to him again with her basket, he was gloomy and didn't strike up a conversation. The following week, as he took his laundry from her, the bookbinder gazed at Marishka attentively and said:

"You've grown thin, Marishka. What's made you grow so thin?"

And then he said: "It's time for me to get a warm kitten to protect me from fear. Marry me, Marishka. Okay?"

****

An old newspaperman and his wife lived kittycorner to the old man's apartment. She went out to work. She was saving money for old age. She felt sorry for Mr. Furtenau.

"All alone like that! He has only the cat and no contact with anyone else. And if the cat dies, what will he do then? It's terrible."

These old people didn't have anyone else either. They didn't even have a cat—they didn't like them.

One evening they heard Mr. Furtenau talking to his cat, and suddenly the old newspaperman remembered: "What orphanage was your niece's son sent to when she died? Hm?"

"What? Are you thinking of taking him out of there? I've just started thinking about that, too."

They found the boy and brought him home. He turned out to be rowdy and mischievous. He sang songs and played tricks. The old people grumbled at him, yelled at him, sometimes even boxed his ears. And above their commotion they could no longer hear Mr. Furtenau talking to his cat.

****

Some newlywed dyers moved from the big city into the small cellar in the old man's apartment house. They had just gotten married and had placed the bride's old mother in a poorhouse. Now they were beginning to settle down and work. All day long they worked cheerfully and in harmony. In the evenings they relaxed and, of course, they heard Mr. Furtenau talking to his cat. They listened to his lonely babble. It sobered them and they stopped laughing.

"What are you always so thoughtful about?" the young dyer asked his wife one day.

Mr. Furtenau's Cat

She was silent.

"Do you know what came into my head?" asked the dyer. "If we moved that large cupboard there would be room to fix up a bed in the corner. Do you follow my drift?"

She remained silent.

"For your mother."

Even then she didn't say anything, only suddenly she began to cry, and then to laugh, and she kissed her husband.

The old woman moved out of the poorhouse and into the corner behind the cupboard. She grumbled, puttered about and fussed, filling their home with the confusion of an old woman. And they could no longer hear Mr. Furtenau talking to his cat.

****

Once again autumn came around. The wind began to blow. The rusty weathervane on the spire of the old belltower began to squeak. It spun around and pecked the moon with its black nose. A dull routine.

Mr. Furtenau stayed at home and didn't go outside for several days. All that the neighbors could hear was him talking to his cat and the cat's "meow" in return.

"Why doesn't he go outside? Maybe he's sick?"

"Well, as long as he's talking to his cat, everything must be all right."

At the end of the week the watchman's wife went up to the old man's apartment to scrub his kitchen. She knocked and knocked, but he didn't respond.

The neighbors became frightened and called a locksmith to break open the door.

Mr. Furtenau was sitting in his armchair, his head drooping. The doctor later said he had died long before, perhaps as many as five days before.

And across from the armchair, in a large cage, perched a parrot—old, bald, featherless, a terrible bird. On seeing people enter, the parrot shrieked in a wild voice: "Peetie! Peetie! Peetie! Want some milk? Meow! Meow!"

The parrot shrieked and fell off of its perch.

It had died of exhaustion.

And the cat that had caused so many amazing things on the church square in the town of Sonnebach—that cat of Mr. Furtenau's had never existed at all.

Don Quixote and the Turgenevan Girl

Zina was acting unusually sweet and affectionate. She expressed delight in her friend's eyelashes, her legs, her stockings, her hairdo, even her teeth, as if she were seeing her for the first time.

"She desperately wants something from me," thought Zoya. "Maybe she lost at cards?"

"How's your poker?" Zoya asked, trying to move her friend closer toward her goal. "Have you played recently?"

"Poker?" Zina repeated. "Oh, I'm so far from all that now! I'll tell you everything later."

She blushed just a bit and began to laugh, but then she fell silent.

"Listen, Zi," said her friend. "It's better to confess right away. It's a new affair, isn't it?"

"Worse!" answered Zina, blushing and beginning to laugh again. "It's worse... I'm in love."

"So what's new?" Zoya asked bluntly.

"Why such an angry tone?" Zina was hurt. "Are you condemning me, Zo? You don't have the right to do that, Zo. If you had a husband like mine, you'd have run away from him long ago."

"What are you complaining about!" said Zoya, exasperated. "Your Vasya's ideal. He's intelligent, kind, and attentive. And so good-looking!"

"Then you can have him, along with all his virtues. Do you hear? But I can't take any more. I'm suffocating..."

"I don't understand." Zoya was puzzled. "Why are you suffocating?"

"Precisely from his virtues. You know, more than anything a husband should be a comrade, someone you can talk to about everything simply and cheerfully, someone who understands a little flirtation, a little joking, all kinds of sweet nonsense. But this idiotic Don Quixote of mine—if I told him something even slightly risqué, his eyes would pop out and he'd keel right over. To him I'm neither a friend nor a wife, but some kind of respected aunt he wouldn't dare take to a girlie show. Well, if he won't dare take me, then I'll go with someone else!"

Zoya was at a loss for words. "How strange all this is! But it must be quite nice to be respected."

"It only seems that way, because you've never experienced it."

Zoya pursed her lips.

"I hope you're not foolish enough to be offended by my words," continued Zina. "Just thank God that no one has ever respected you. It's a terrible thing—a person close to you who respects you. It's really dreadful! I'm young. I love laughter and good jokes. You know, my idiot is afraid that one of those 'vulgar little books' will somehow fall into my hands. He imagines I'll be dreadfully shocked. I really don't know why he's so convinced that I'm a holy touch-me-not."

"You could explain his delusion to him."

"Why destroy illusions? If he's happy that he wound up with a wife to his liking, why ruin his life? It's much simpler to create your own private life according to your own tastes and ask your dear friend Zo to come to your aid. Hm?"

"I knew you were leading up to something. That's why you're so affectionate today. Well, what do you need?"

Zina hesitated, smacked her lips, moved a bit closer to Zoya, and began to implore in a whisper: "Help me, Zo. You do understand? It's a shame to miss this opportunity. Vasya finally roused himself to go out to dinner and a movie with some old friend who's just arrived in town. But I thought I'd tell him I've arranged to spend the evening with you. Is that all right with you? You won't give me away?"

Zoya frowned.

"Actually, my dear, it's absolutely impossible."

"What!" Zina exclaimed with indignation. "Why is it suddenly impossible?"

"First of all, because I don't want to help deceive someone as worthy as your husband, and secondly, because it simply isn't convenient for me."

"Now there's a real friend! Why is it so inconvenient?"

"I'm going out this evening."

"So?"

"He could call and find no one at home."

"Why on earth would he call? And if it comes to that, we could always say we were at the movies."

"Then you still have to be sneaky and slink around. No. I respect him too much to take on such a vile role."

"I never thought there was so much meanness in you," Zina said bitterly. "If I had known, I never would have turned to you for help."

Both were silent, sulking.

"Why do you need these alibis, anyway, since he himself is going out? Make it look like you stayed home all evening, and that's all there is to it."

"And if he calls?"

"You can say that you went out to mail a letter."

"How smart you are! All right, I'll tell him I stayed home. After all, I'm not going out for long. I only promised to have dinner with my friend. Oh, he's so amusing, I'll have so much fun! Now don't get me wrong, Zo, I love Vasya very much. If only he understood me a little better and didn't carry on with his silly nonsense! You know, it's not a real life we share, but some kind of poetry recital to the accompaniment of an Aeolian harp and saccharine stars. And what I love is fried sausage with garlic! What can I do? You understand, I appreciate Vasya very much and wouldn't trade him for anyone, but sometimes I just feel like howling. Why is he so stiff? He's a sweet, intelligent, noble man, but there's not a drop of character in him. He doesn't feel life, he doesn't understand its brilliant moments. He doesn't even know they exist."

She stopped and thought.

"So how about it, Zoechka? Zo, dear? You think I should just say that I'll be home all evening?"

****

Zoya herself opened the door at his ring.

He came in so cheerfully, so impetuously, so full of joy, that even the glass pendants on the chandelier seemed to ring in response.

"Ssh, Vasya, what's the matter with you?" Zoya chided, though she couldn't help laughing along with him.

"You can't imagine how hard it was to leave!" he gasped, kissing both her hands in turn. "I thought I'd tell Zina I was having dinner with a friend. Clever, hm? But she suddenly declared that, in that case, she was going to spend the evening with you. How do you like that? I really didn't know what to do. How could I possibly dissuade her? All I could do was advise her, 'Find out first whether your Zina will be home tonight, otherwise you'll go traipsing over there for nothing and be upset if she's not in. Call her on the phone,' I said. Well, she decided that since she'd be somewhere not far from you this afternoon, she'd just drop in. And when she came home with a headache, she decided she'd be better off just going to bed. So everything turned out famously, after all!"

"What a beast you are! You're glad your wife has a headache. Really, doesn't that make you a beast?"

"Well, it's nothing serious—just a slight headache. If it were serious, that would be a different matter. But let's get down to the question at hand. Where shall we go? I'm in a boisterous mood. 'I could just throw back my shoulders and swing my arms!"* Zoika! Let's go have dinner. Let's eat at some real gypsyish place. Okay? Well? Look lively! Hat! Wait a minute, put some lipstick on me first."

"On you? On your lips? What kind of nonsense is that?"

"Put it on with your lips, you silly, muddle-headed goose! Mmm, how good it is to be alive! How grand life is!"

****

As often happens, when people want to talk they head for a restaurant with music. The music interferes with their conversation and drowns out their voices. They have to ask each question three times or else wait for a break in the music. Often they become impatient and irritable. Nevertheless, when people want to talk, they invariably choose a restaurant with music.

Zoya efficiently found a table close to the stage. They sat down.

She looked with pleasure at the radiant face of her friend's husband.

"Well, Cat-Vaska**, are you happy?"

"Terribly happy." The look on his face was that of a dog wagging its tail in every direction. "My, I'm happy!"

They were in high spirits. They laughed loudly, drank quite a bit.

"Isn't it wonderful to be alive!"

"Not bad at all," answered Zoya. "I just wish it were like this more often."

Vasya was silent and looked at his watch.

"What? You're being drawn home already?" Zoya asked sarcastically.

"No, we still have time. I'll say we went to a movie and then for a walk. Because the night is so lovely."

"So lovely? It's raining cats and dogs out there."

"Really!" He was surprised. "It's lucky you called my attention to that fact. I'll tell her we stopped in at a café, then. On an impulse."

"Of course. On impulse things turn out best of all."

"Maybe. Although once I lied so much on impulse that, frankly, I frightened myself. But she didn't even notice, the poor thing."

"You feel very sorry for her?" Zoya asked sympathetically.

Vasya turned his gaze away.

---

*This line is from Alexei Koltsov's poem "The Reaper." (Trans.)

**Vaska (a diminutive of the name Vasilii, as is Vasya) is the cat's name in the Russian fable by Ivan Krylov "The Cat and the Cook" (1812). (Trans.)

"She's a wonderful, dear person," he said. "I love her very, very much. But we're so poorly suited to each other. Look, you know both of us well. Tell me—could there possibly be any greater contrast than between her and me? I'm an utterly vulgar person, I love this base little life of ours. I'm frivolous—live and let live! But Zina is a Turgenevan girl, pure and timid, just like a little fawn. I'm always afraid of startling her, always on the alert, always careful, always afraid I might let something fall with a bang in front of her. Zo, darling, you're an intelligent woman, you understand. You can't imagine how all this oppresses me sometimes. How happy I'd be if Zina not only loved me, but knew me and understood me, too! But she'll never understand me and never forgive me. I'd even agree to her being unfaithful—fleetingly, of course, nothing serious—if only it would help us to understand each other better and bring us closer together... But why are you laughing, Zo? Aren't you listening to my bitter confession?"

Zoya was trying to restrain herself, but she could not hold back her laughter. Her chin and cheeks quivered. Tears came to her eyes.

"Vasenka! Darling! Forgive me! I... my dentist told me the funniest story today. Of course, it doesn't have anything to do with.. Well, anyway, there's a certain couple among his patients, a husband and wife. The husband had a set of false teeth made in secret from his wife. And the wife hides the fact from him that she herself has false teeth. Both asked the dentist not to give them away. You can imagine the inconvenience this must cause them. Each has to sneak around, always locking the other out when performing the toilette. The dentist says, 'It's in my hands to set this matter straight, to call them both in together and disclose their secrets. How that would simplify their lives! But I can't do it. I'm bound by my word.'"

Vasenka was startled by the story. "Why did you remember such nonsense?"

"I don't really know," Zoya answered gaily. "Anyway, we'd better run. Poor Zinushka has been waiting long enough."

Two Affairs with Foreigners

The twilight was serene at the waning of the day. Automobile headlights played along the wall of the room, horns cried out, a streetcar jangled. Like an awl, the bell of the neighboring movie theater pierced the ear.

But the twilight was nonetheless serene for the two women sitting cross-legged on the wobbly couch, because another day with all its anxieties and troubles had come to an end, and in these two or three hours left before bedtime they could allow themselves not to think about or worry about anything.

Heart-to-heart conversations are often carried on in serene twilight like this. It's not comfortable to walk around in the growing darkness; you have to sit quietly. Even your thoughts become more concentrated, no longer skipping from topic to topic. The most habitual chatterboxes lose their inspiration, becoming simpler and more sincere.

At moments like this young people talk readily about death. The middle-aged, about love. And old people talk about hope.

The two women who had crossed their legs on the wobbly couch were no longer young. Therefore they talked about love.

"It's all over for me now," one of them sighed.

If the room had been brighter, we could have seen a tired face, dim eyes and shoulders wrapped up in a fluffy grey shawl, always a bit torn at the shoulders—a shawl nevertheless comfortable, smelling of perfume and cigarettes—the traditional shawl of a grieving Russian woman.

"Don't exaggerate, Natasha," replied the other. "You're still young. Who knows?"

"Young?" Natasha said with a bitter laugh. "No, my dear, after what I've lived through, I feel like I'm seventy. But it's my own fault. I should never have betrayed Grisha's memory."

"How many years were you married to Grisha?"

"Years? Years! Five weeks. We met just before the evacuation. Got married right away. Five weeks later he joined the campaign. We never saw each other again. He was so very sweet..."

"Yes, for five weeks you can put up with anything."

"I'm not so sure about that," Natasha said in a hurt tone.

"And what ever happened to your fiancé, that Frenchman of yours? I really don't remember a thing about it. I didn't see you much when he was courting you, then suddenly I heard the engagement was off. Did he fall out of love with you or something?"

"No, no. He swears he didn't fall out of love. It's just that his parents wouldn't let him marry me. It's a very complicated story," sighed Natasha.

"I survived a complicated story, too, but I don't sigh, I laugh. Did you ever try to shoot yourself? Take poison?"

"No, of course not—what a sin!"

"You see! And here you're sighing. I went so far as to take poison, but whenever I think about it, I can't help laughing. Oh, how sweet it was, how dear!"

"What's so sweet about poisoning yourself?"

"There's little good in that, of course. It made me very sick. Yet it was because I poisoned myself that everything turned out so amusing. But I'll tell my story later. You first."

"Okay. Only where to begin . . . Well, as you already know, I was working in a hat shop, where I got to know Madame Ruzhot, Marie. She was very sweet. We became great friends and decided to open a new shop together. Her husband was also a fine person, an engineer. At first our business didn't go too badly. We were inseparable. We spent our days in the workshop and our little store, evenings we went to the movies or played cards. I ate dinner with the Ruzhots, so I didn't have to bother with housekeeping. Well, one of Ruzhot's colleagues, a Monsieur Emile, used to visit them quite often. To make a long story short, this Emile fell desperately in love with me. He didn't particularly appeal to me at first—he seemed like such a shallow, banal type. But little by little he began to arouse my interest. And soon we were seeing each other almost every day. He expressed his love so persistently, so ardently, with so much rapture, that involuntarily I began to be more attentive to him."

"Exactly! Exactly!" her listener interrupted.

"What do you mean, 'exactly'?" The storyteller was surprised.

"Nothing, really. It just came out."

"So I began to be more attentive to him. And here Marie poured grease on the fire: '*Pauvre* Emile. He's dying,' she says, '*pauvre* Emile. He's such a wonderful person and he's well off, and you're all alone—who's going to take care of you? You should marry *pauvre* Emile.' And every evening after dinner, Emile demanded this marriage. His persistence began to touch me. He began to appeal to me."

"Exactly, exactly!" her listener interjected.

"What do you mean, 'exactly'? What are you getting at?"

"Nothing, nothing, it just popped out again."

"Marie's husband tried to persuade me, too. And eventually I noticed that this Emile was beginning to appeal to me quite a lot. But all the same I couldn't decide on marriage yet. I wanted to test both myself and him. Really only myself, because to doubt *him* would have been ridiculous. He suffered, he was in bliss . . . God knows what else—a mixture of both Romeo and Juliet, if you can imagine it! I tormented him for a long time. Finally I said: 'It seems to me I'll be able to love you.' And then—you can't imagine it—he cried aloud. Out of delight he rushed to kiss Marie. He didn't dare kiss me, so he kissed her. It was both funny and touching. Right then and there he decided to write to his parents in Paris and arrange to introduce me. Marie's husband explained to me that since his parents were well-to-do, he couldn't marry without their approval."

"They always involve their parents in these things!" the listener interrupted again, immediately adding, "Nothing, nothing. That just popped out."

"Emile's parents turned out to be very nice—old-fashioned, somehow, and delicate, touching, particularly his mother. She adored me at first sight. We spent entire days together. She'd sit with us in the shop, or I'd go to her place. She was so sincere and so sensitive that she understood everything. And she liked the fact that I didn't give Emile my consent right away, that I wanted to test both myself and him first. She was such a darling that I simply fell in love with her and even shed a few tears when she left. We didn't part for long, though, because she promised to return for the wedding in a month. My Emile exulted, he shone, he simply radiated delight. The dear Ruzhots could not have been happier for us. Marie helped me with the wedding arrangements, gave me gifts, and delighted in my happiness.

"Well, one day, one damned beautiful day, the two of us were sitting with Monsieur Ruzhot, waiting for Marie to come to breakfast. I went into her bedroom to powder my nose and saw a little box lying on the table. The box was half open and a letter was sticking out of it. The paper was blue, just like some Emile had. The handwriting was just like Emile's, too. Involuntarily I looked at it and saw that it really was his handwriting. Of course, this didn't surprise me in the least, because they were such old friends—why shouldn't he write to her? But as ill luck would have it, in the line clearly visible to me my name was written: '*Pauvre* Natasha', I read, and I became interested. Why was I suddenly '*pauvre*'? Curiosity destroyed Eve. I carried the box into a corner, took the letter out, and read it. The contents of the letter were such that there could be no doubts whatsoever. This same '*pauvre* Emile,' this fiancé so madly and happily in love, had been carrying on the most obvious affair with my dear friend Marie, and under my very nose. The affair was quite fresh, all of about ten days old.

" 'Be careful,' begged my tender fiancé, 'that *pauvre* Natasha, whom I love so much, is not distressed by our liaison.'

"All of this was so unexpected, so absurd, that I... I don't know what happened to me. I lost consciousness. Whether I lay there for a long time, I don't know, but when I opened my eyes, I saw Monsieur Ruzhot standing next to me, reading that damned letter with great interest. I wanted to stand up, but I couldn't. My legs were paralyzed.

"He read the letter and turned to me. " 'Darling,' he said, 'how you frightened me! Do you often fall into a faint?'

" 'Give it to me, give me that letter!' I shouted. 'Don't you dare read it!'

"He raised his brows, surprised: 'Do you mean you fainted because of this nonsense?'

"He embraced me, lifted me up, set me down on the couch, stroked my head, and kissed me. But I burst into tears and cried. How could I live now? Everything had crashed down around me.

"He just laughed. 'Nonsense,' he said. 'Get a little angry, it's good for you, then forget it.'

"But I was indignant. 'How can you say that! After all, he was unfaithful to me with your own wife!'

"He just waved his hand. 'All the better. He was unfaithful to you with my wife, so you can be unfaithful to him with me. Then everyone will be happy.'

"At that point I began to bawl in complete hysteria. Then I ran away.

"I locked myself in my house and didn't go out for a week. I wrote letters to everyone. To Emile a rejection, to Marie a reproach, to Ruzhot a curse. But my main letter was to the old woman, Emile's mother. I explained everything to her and said farewell to her with sincere emotion. I never received an answer.

"After a week I had to go to the shop—there was no getting around it. Business. Marie and I encountered each other with some constraint. She was slightly mocking, as if I had behaved ridiculously over nothing. Little by little she dissuaded me. She mentioned, in passing, that Emile wanted to shoot himself, that in general, reasonable women don't act like I had, that one just doesn't fall into a faint with a compromising letter in her hands, that it's indiscreet, even dishonorable, but that she loves me and therefore forgives the embarrassment I caused her, but that, of course, after my (my!) dreadful behavior our friendship can no longer continue. Then Emile appeared. He sobbed, beat his head against the wall—first the back of his head, then his forehead. I was implacable. But, alas, not for long! He was somehow able to convince me. I forgave him. Everything got going again as if right from the start, but then a letter

Two Affairs with Foreigners

came from his mother. She'd addressed the letter to him—because with a woman like me she had nothing to talk about.

"In the letter to her son she categorically forbade him to marry me, because if I was capable of making such an uproar over nonsense, then what would there be in the future? What kind of life would that be? 'She will constantly be fainting and compromising your friends, including women respected by everyone.'

"Emile was very sad. He said he was counting on the mitigating influence of time. His mother would think better of it and change her mind. But of course, while his mother was thinking better of it, he married someone else."

"That's all?" asked the listener. "Really, my affair was much more amusing. Let me tell you about it. I'll tell you, only it all seems so silly now. If the room weren't so dark, I'd be embarrassed even to look at you."

"No matter. We're old friends. I won't turn on the lamp. Let's sit in the dark a little longer. So who did you have an affair with? A Frenchman, too?"

"No. You'll never guess! A Rumanian."

"A Rumanian—how strange!"

"And how! A real tragedy. Ha-ha-ha!"

"A tragedy, and you laugh!" cried her friend. "Or maybe you're hysterical?"

"Darling, if you only knew how funny it was! I poisoned myself, you know."

"What's so funny about that?"

Had the room been brighter, we would see that the one who had poisoned herself was a plump brunette with lively black, bulging eyes and neat little curls. She was wearing an inexpensive, but stylish dress and lots of make-up. She had plucked brows and smoothed-back hair. She seemed calm and satisfied. If the room had been brighter, we'd look at her and think: "She's lying. That type doesn't poison herself."

"So what's the joke?" her friend repeated. "If you poisoned yourself, you obviously suffered."

"And how! Ha-ha-ha! That's why it's funny—because I suffered."

"Well, tell me! We'll laugh together," her friend said ironically.

"Here's how it was, my dear. I was working at the time for Madame Verfluch at the *Institut de Beauté*. We worked well together. That kind of business is very psychological, you know. You probably think it's easy to apply make-up—just dab it on and that's that. But no, my dear, that's not quite enough. Especially if the client is an elderly veteran of numerous heartfelt disappointments. Heart-to-heart conversation is essential. Still, when you pluck her brows, it's okay to be silent, because the plucking hurts and she's busy groaning. When you clean her pores, it's also not exactly a timely moment for baring one's soul. That job is almost medical, if you know what I mean. But when it comes to the *beauté* itself—cream, lotion, rouges, powders—every woman's soul opens up. Just why this is so, I can't really explain, I only know it's a fact. You can ask any facial masseuse. You'd simply marvel at what they tell sometimes, these clients. You'd think they wouldn't reveal such things under torture! If I wrote it all down, it would fill several volumes. And what volumes they would be!

"Anyway, I had a certain older client, a rather quiet type. I'm ashamed to say that I thought she was quiet simply because of her age.

"The old woman was small and frail, with a sharp nose. Her cheeks were taut and sewn to her temples, and the skin under her chin was pinned back behind her ears. She was a good customer, she wasn't stingy with the tips. Not that she handled the money—her servant paid her account. As soon as the session was over, this servant would approach, wrap her up in a fur coat and carry her off to her car. Right in his arms. All this *beauté* greatly tired her. She used to just lie there—I'd be glueing on false eyelashes—and she'd open her mouth a bit (she had a terrible black mouth, and the skin on her cheeks covered her like a book binding) and she'd begin to snore. She would fall asleep from weariness. This lady led a very tiring life. Visits, fittings, teas, dinners, concerts, sports. Yes, sports. She played golf. Just think! At her age, bringing such torment on herself!

"One day she showed up in a peculiar mood. She was keyed up, she smiled, she put on airs. She ordered every kind of cream and rouge. She was going to America.

"Suddenly, right out of the blue, she grabs my hand. 'Darling!' she says. 'If you only knew how I hate to leave! Particularly now. But my husband insists . . . Some sort of business. It's probably all nonsense. And I want to stay *here* now. Understand?'

"Of course one must always understand a client like that. I sighed and said: 'Oh, I do understand!'

"But what it was I had to understand, I didn't for the life of me know.

"The old woman began to tremble. 'I met him two days ago,' she said, 'and decided to invite him to manage my affairs. Oh, if you knew! If you only knew! He's not just some young boy from a dance hall. He's nobility itself. He's intellect! He's heart! He's brunet. And here I haven't even managed to make arrangements with him as to his responsibilities, when I have to cast everything aside and rush off to America. But I'll return, I'll return very soon.'

"She hadn't even finished pouring out her soul to me when there was a knock at our room and we were told that a Monsieur Pierre wanted to see my client.

"She gasped for breath. 'It's him! It's him!'

"Into the room came a young man, rather handsome, only somehow too-too. You know what I mean: skin too white, cheeks too ruddy, raspberry-red lips, black hair almost blue, perfect brows—really like some kind of gaudy Ukrainian painting. But handsome all the same. Terribly polite. He had brought the old woman tickets from some lady or other. He'd found out she was here, and because the matter was urgent, had taken it upon himself, and so on and so forth.

"My old woman simply began to vibrate. He took her by the arm and whirled her away.

"But if he whirled her away, what did I care?

"Well, about two days later this same Pierre appeared and came right over to me. He excused himself very respectfully and asked whether Madame Wood had perhaps forgotten her gloves.

" 'Hasn't she left?' I asked.

" 'Yes,' he said, she had left the very next morning and had instructed him to find out about her gloves.

"I ordered the porter to look for them, to ask the cashier.

"Meanwhile, Monsieur Pierre watched me, smiling strangely.

" 'It must be dreadfully boring for you here,' he said, 'since you have such an exceptional appearance.'

"I assumed a fitting air. 'Not in the least,' I said. 'I like the work very much.'

"And he says: 'Faced constantly with such weariness and old age, it is essential to be entertained. Otherwise you could completely overload your nerves. Perhaps,' he said, 'you will allow me to have you in mind with respect to the movies.'

"I agreed—with great formality, however.

"He was terribly pleased and called to the porter: 'Don't bother looking any more, I already found them.'

"Then I understood he had made the whole thing up in order to see me. I confess, this really got to me. 'Here's a man who circulates in such magnificent American society,' I thought, 'and suddenly he reacts like that to my appearance.'

"Well, things went on. He began to see me often. And it was constantly, 'Do you love me, do you love me?'

"I, in our Russian style, said neither yes nor no. I was full of mystery. He was so tormented! He was completely worn out.

" 'Elena,' he said, 'you're a saint. You're Saint Elena and I will die, like Bonaparte.'

"For about two months I kept him on the hook. Finally I said: 'It's more yes than no.'

"Of course, out of sheer joy he lost his head completely. 'In that case,' he said, 'allow me to bring you some pastry.'

"He brought me the pastry, but in his distraction, he ate all of it.

"Incidentally, it came out that his last name—it's hard to believe!—was Chicken. Maybe in Rumanian that's a very chic name. Maybe in Rumanian it's like Musin-Pushkin, Shakhovskoy, and Gagarin. How can we tell? Of course it's terrible, but I had fallen so in love with him that I even swallowed this Chicken.

"He began pressuring me to marry him. Here the name of Chicken was not a cheerful thought for me, but I was so much in love with him that I barely gave it a second thought.

"He was involved with the stock market. It seems he didn't make bad money. But as far as that goes, I'm not really sure.

"Already he was coming to see me like a real suitor, giving me small presents in a most domestic spirit. He gave me an electric iron. Very nice of him! We hid it together in the hall cupboard.

"Now everything is approaching its blissful conclusion... One day, I recalled our first meeting. I said to him: 'You know, Pierrusha, I think that old witch was in love with you and had particular designs on you.'

"He blushed in indignation. 'Where did you get that idea? You just made that up.'

"I told him how she had hinted to me about someone she'd just met.

"He questioned me in great detail. He was obviously disturbed by my assumption. I tried to smooth things over with a joke, but he became distracted and thoughtful. I'd obviously offended him deeply. And imagine, from that very moment it was as though something had snapped. He began to come over less often. He didn't say a word about the wedding. As you might expect, I jumped on him right then and there. The further he pulled away, the more painful it was for me—as if he had caught hold of one of my teeth with a wire. What didn't I do! I feigned indifference, I cried, I sang Gypsy romances. Nothing worked. My Chicken withdrew from me. In the end I wore myself out.

"Meanwhile, my little old American returned. She came to me to make her beautiful again. She was cheerful and gave me one hundred francs.

"I said to my colleagues: 'Our old woman is romping with a young filly.'

"The receptionist laughed. 'She has a gigolo,' she said. 'That ruddy one who rushed in here to see her before she left. I'm always running into them in her car, and I saw them twice in a restaurant.'

"I could barely wait out my hours, barely drag myself home. I wrote to him: 'When you read these lines, come, and silently I will say farewell to you.'

"I sent the note by pneumatic post. Then I got out a jar of rat poison, rolled the poison into a little pill, and swallowed it. I shrieked and swallowed it. I didn't even feel regret for life. 'He'll come,' I thought, 'and then he'll understand what it means to say a silent farewell.'

"But the rat poison was no good. For a whole day and night it wrenched me apart. And the bastard came only after several days. He sat in profile, telling me some kind of nonsense about his parents not liking their children to marry. I cried—I overflowed.

"Then he stood up and said that my image would always be before his mind's eye, but that he was too noble to make me unhappy by subjecting me to the wrath of his family.

"He left dramatically, covering his eyes with his hand.

"I threw the window open wide and readied myself. As soon as he came out of the entrance, I was going to fling myself onto the street. So be it. Just like that.

"But for some reason he was lingering in the hall. I heard the cupboard door squeak. What could that mean? Then the outside door clicked shut. He was gone! But whatever had he done? Why did he open the cupboard?

"I dashed into the hall, opened the cupboard . . . Goodness gracious! You know . . . you know it's almost impossible to believe this! He took back his iron! His i-i-iron!

"Believe it or not, I sat right down on the floor. I laughed and laughed, and how easy I began to feel, how relieved!

" 'Lord!' I said. 'How wonderful it is to live in this world!' Even now, when I think of it, ha-ha-ha, now that I recall it, I'll probably laugh till morning. His iron! His i-i-iron! I would have crashed onto the street, my skull in smithereens, and in his hands the i-i-iron! What a picture!

"Yes, my dear, there are some things in life you couldn't imagine even if you tried."

The Choice of a Cross

There's a novella called "The Choice of a Cross," where a man becomes exhausted under the burden of his cross. He cries out in protest and starts scrounging for a different cross to bear. But no matter which one he tries on, each turns out to be worse than the cross before. It's either too long or too wide or cuts too sharply into his shoulder. Finally he rests his decision on the basis of comfort and takes back his own cross, the one he had first rejected.

It's because of the following incident that we are reminded of this novella.

****

Ermilov respected his Anna very much. She was a convenient wife to have—solicitous and intelligent. But when he met Zoya Erbel, he was amazed that he could have lived so many years with such a prosaic creature as Anna.

It wasn't that Anna was bad-looking. She was big and broad-boned, with large hands and feet and a fresh face. She dressed simply, preferring English blouses, shoes with flat heels, and masculine gloves. She didn't wear make-up or perfume. Everything in the world was clear and simple to her. Mystics were unbalanced types, being in love was simply the instinctive neurosis of the sexes, and as for poetry—"not bad, if it has content."

Anna was never over-indulgent towards her husband. She didn't call him by any affectionate or pet names, but to make up for that she looked after him very attentively to make sure he had everything he needed. She took a great interest in his digestion and appetite, she made him do exercises and take up sports.

But Ermilov didn't like sports, exercises tired him, and after four years, Anna tired him, too.

He was bored with her.

He was bored to find the house always in order, everything scrubbed and cleaned, nothing superfluous.

"Just like a military hospital," he'd grumble.

His first visit to the Erbels was by chance, on business. He was immediately struck, then moved, by the condition of the room where he had to await his host.

The table was piled high with heaps of newspapers and magazines in great disorder, as though someone had rooted through them with no other purpose in mind. On top of the papers lay an open box revealing nibbled bits of candy. Out from under them peeked something pink. The garter and bow from a girdle hung right down over the edge of the table, while a wide-open purse gaped out at him from the disarray.

The furniture in the room was arranged helter-skelter, with an armchair turning its back to the table and one of the chairs facing right up to the wall.

From the next room Ermilov could hear a ringing female voice. It sang a strange little song, melancholy in content yet cheerful in tune:

> "No money, no money,
> Absolutely no money."

Then the same voice cried out in despair: "Shurka! Kvik dragged away my stocking again! Shurka! Look behind the door. *I* can't—there's a stranger out there."

A discontented bass voice grumbled dimly in reply. Then once again the female voice said decisively: "Well, I'll go myself then. What can I do? These are my only stockings, you know. The dog has stolen all the others and torn them up. What? Well, so what? He won't eat me up, this businessman of yours."

The door opened cautiously, and a young woman in pink pajamas, dishevelled and embarrassed, came out into the room.

"Excuse me," she said. "My husband will be right out. He's writing. I forgot my . . ."

She quickly ran her eyes along the floor, glanced at the table, and catching sight of the pink garter, was sincerely pleased: "Oh, so that's where it is! I'm so glad I found it."

And turning towards the door she had appeared from, she yelled: "Shurka! Don't bother looking for the girdle, I found it. And the stocking's on it."

She gave Ermilov the most genteel smile, pulled her girdle— from which a stocking really was hanging—out from under a magazine, waved her hand affably, as if from the window of a departing train, and slammed the door behind her. After a few minutes Erbel came out, quite tall and perplexed, searching helplessly with his eyes for something. Evidently he had lost his necktie, for with one hand he was holding back the collar of his shirt.

"Excuse me! Oh, for Christ's sake!" he said with embarrassment. "There's such chaos here. I'll be ready right away and we can go next door to a cafe. It will be more comfortable to talk there."

The Choice of a Cross

He spread his hands in a gesture of helplessness, glanced behind the couch, and left the room.

A minute later his despairing howl resounded beyond the door: "Why the hell did you tie my necktie onto the dog! What an idiotic thing to do! My God!"

In answer, a new recitation burst forth:

"Because my soul has no name
And because my lips are unkissed!"

Finally Erbel came out completely dressed. He fussed about in the hall looking for his hat, but soon spotted it under the table. He shook it, blew on it, and opened the door to the staircase.

They were already on the street walking along the sidewalk when a ringing voice sang out above:

"You tenderly squint your eyes at the skies,
At the intoxicating, ringing azure . . ."

Erbel angrily quickened his pace, but Ermilov raised his head to see a pink figure on the balcony of the second floor. At that moment something wet flicked painfully across his nose. It was a flower thrown by the pink figure, no doubt snatched from a vase where it had rotted long ago because it was completely slimy and limp and foul-smelling. Nevertheless Ermilov picked it up.

"It's not for you," the ringing voice cried from above. "It's for my mean Shurka, for my beloved angel."

The "beloved angel" turned around and with a beastly grimace hissed to Ermilov: "Throw that crap away! You've stained your whole jacket."

Ermilov walked along and smiled. "What an amazing woman," he thought. "You can't get bored with one like that! Everything in her sings, everything in her rings . . ."

****

Erbel gave his wife her due. She was young, cheerful and carefree. No matter how bad their finances were, she never whined or reproached him for his failures.

But on the other hand, there was no use expecting support or help from her. The house was in total disorder—business letters, money, and other things disappeared without a trace. There was no set time for sleeping or for meals.

She had the best intentions, and seeing that her disorderliness tormented her husband, she acquired a budget book, on the first page of which Erbel read with interest: "Given to me for expenses: 600 francs. Spent 585. 100 remaining, but I can't find them. Have only 15."

"Zoyechka," he called his wife. "What does this mean?"

"This?" Zoya asked in a business-like way. "It's subtraction."

"What kind of subtraction?"

"You're so carping! I did the subtraction in the margin especially for you to see, just so you wouldn't find fault with me. Now look. From 600 I subtracted 585, and 100 remained. But I can't find them."

"Wait a minute, why 100?" Erbel was surprised.

"What do you mean, why? Look for yourself: five from zero is zero."

"Why zero?"

"What are all these 'whys' for? It's obvious why. Zero represents a number which has exactly nothing. So how on earth can you take something away from nothing? How can it give you something to subtract?"

"You've just got to borrow, you know."

"Borrow? From whom?"

"From the next number."

"How strange! But look, there's a zero there, too. It doesn't have anything either."

"So it will borrow from the next number," her husband assured her.

"And you actually imagine that that number will lend him something! This second zero goes borrowing only to end up giving it away to that first beggar. Where in the world do such things ever happen? It's funny just listening to you."

"I see that you simply can't do subtraction."

"If it were just something mechanical, of course I could do it. But when I have to think about it, then all these borrowings from some poor old zeroes are organically repulsive to me. Borrow them yourself, if you want to, but spare me . . . Like here, you gave a thousand francs. Three zeroes. A jolly crowd. And they'll all go begging from that poor one! And he's nothing more than a one himself. Well . . . do as you like, I've had enough."

Erbel sighed, took his hat, dejectedly brushed the dust from it with his sleeve, and left the apartment.

The first time he saw Anna, Emilov's wife, he was smitten.

"What a quiet, sweet woman! How clear, pure, and simple everything about her is. She eases your soul."

The Choice of a Cross

He stayed at the Ermilovs a long time, not wanting to go home. But finally he had to go, and when he entered his hallway, tripping over a wide-open suitcase and hearing a thunderous recitation coming from the bedroom, he almost began to cry.

Two days later Erbel was expecting Ermilov at his house at exactly three o'clock, but he returned home around two to find his new friend already there. Ermilov was sitting astride a chair, ecstatically feeding the dog chocolates, and Zoya, with pajama legs rolled up above her knees, was dancing a sailor's jig in front of him.

On seeing Erbel, Ermilov was dreadfully embarrassed, and in confusion he began to explain that he had come early hoping to find Erbel at home—that way they would have had more time for business.

Erbel could not understand his confusion at all.

The next day Erbel went to Ermilov's "to find out the address of a good copyist," just at the time when the master of the house was usually away. But on this occasion Ermilov happened to be there. He in turn was not in the least surprised by Erbel's visit.

"How did you sense that I didn't go to work today?" he asked with complete sincerity.

Erbel mumbled something, and when Anna suggested that they go to the pool together to swim, he agreed so quickly and with such delight that Ermilov looked at him suspiciously.

"I would never have thought that you liked such nonsense!"

Anna was even more charming in the water than in her usual environment. She was fresh, strong, quick and quietly cheerful. Guiding Erbel with a sure hand, powerful yet gentle, she taught him to dive and jump from the board.

They decided to swim every day. Sometimes they went to a pond to go boating. It was all wonderful, and the further it went, the more wonderful it became.

Erbel always brought Anna home. Then they would have dinner together, and often he stayed all evening.

Ermilov was almost never at home.

But one day it happened that someone was supposed to call Erbel on business, so he went home earlier than usual. Opening the door with his key and glancing into the living room, he could not immediately grasp what was going on.

The room was half-dark. Zoya was sitting at the wide-open window. She was sitting on something tall, her arm strangely raised and bent at the elbow. Swaying back and forth, she was reciting:

"Love me without reflection,
Without anguish, without fatal thought..."

Erbel peered with interest and saw that the tall thing Zoya was sitting on was someone's knees, and that Zoya's bent arm was embracing someone's shoulders.

Wanting to know more precisely what was going on, Erbel turned on the light. Zoya jumped up, revealing the confused and dishevelled Ermilov, who stood up clutching his head.

Erbel made a reassuring gesture and said in a gentlemanly tone: "Please, don't be embarrassed. Excuse me for disturbing you."

He turned and went out, very pleased with himself. He didn't feel the slightest bit hurt. Only surprised.

"To be unfaithful to me with such a dolt! To be unfaithful to *her* with such a nobody!"

Shrugging his shoulders and forgetting about the business call—he was hardly up to that now—he flew to Anna.

Anna took the news rather indifferently.

"Well, they're both exceptionally unbalanced types," she said. "Almost off the deep end. Immoderate. You know I don't like anything harmful. Everything should be without excess. So you'd better leave now because if Nikolai returns, meeting him here might result in excess."

Disregarding the unpleasant impression produced by the twice-repeated word "excess," Erbel found within himself the strength to take Anna by the hand and say, "Anna, I'm glad it happened this way. I'm glad that you and I are free now. Do you understand?"

Anna understood.

"Yes," she said in a business-like way. "Of course, there is convenience of sorts in this. I mean your attraction to me. But on the other hand, all this disturbs the calm course of life."

"Anna, I love you!" he cried. "I want to unite our course, that is our lives, that is the course of our life. Pure and simple!"

****

So everything was arranged.

Erbel moved into Ermilov's apartment with delight. Ermilov obediently moved in with Zoya.

And time passed.

****

Exactly how the time passed, we don't know, but after about three years Ermilov had to go see Erbel on business.

They arranged things over the telephone, and at the appointed time Ermilov entered the familiar doorway.

The Choice of a Cross

Surprised at his mood, he climbed the stairs.

"It's as if I feel regret," he thought.

The familiar hallway. Everything as it was. Everything just as clean and bright as before and nothing superfluous. Only there on the peg hung a strange man's overcoat. Still, just before their separation he was used to seeing a strange coat on the rack. Only then he had been indifferent, while now for some reason he was sad.

Anna met him, as strong and fresh as before.

"Hello, Nikolai," she said quietly. "You'll have to wait a minute. Aleksandr has never learned to be punctual. In general he's the type that refuses to give in to the standards of society."

Ermilov sat down in the armchair which had once been his favorite.

Anna looked at her watch.

"In twenty-five minutes we can drink some tea."

He remembered her exactness in making schedules.

"It seemed rather dry," he thought. "But on the other hand, how convenient!"

Erbel did not return at the appointed time.

"Call home," Anna advised. "He probably got everything mixed up and went to your place. Aleksandr is confusion personified," she added with irritation.

But Ermilov didn't want to call home.

"Then stay for dinner," Anna suggested. "I'm glad to see you."

He was surprised and pleased at the invitation. He ate with pleasure at the well-laid table, then sat down in his favorite armchair and automatically reached his hand out for a newspaper.

Anna began to inquire about his affairs in a business-like and intelligent way.

He experienced the feeling of a man returning home after a busy but tiring and boring trip. He wanted to stretch out, yawn, and say with a satisfied smile: "Well, now I can relax. I'll get down to work later."

Ermilov returned home late. While still on the stairs he heard Zoya singing some nonsense and winced in disgust.

"She's not a woman, she's a birdbrained fool."

He entered the room and stopped short.

Zoya was sitting on the couch, Erbel on the rug, resting his head on her knees and embracing her waist with both hands.

"Please, don't be embarrassed," Ermilov said calmly. "Excuse me for disturbing you."

He turned around and went out.

He went out and returned to Anna.

And all the way home he tried to remember where he had heard the proud and noble phrase he'd just uttered with such style.
But he couldn't remember.

Points of View

It was an ordinary Parisian Sunday at the beginning of summer. Neither hot nor cold.

As always, the people of Paris were hurrying along the roads away from the city, by all possible means—bus and car and tram and train.

Vasily Petrovich Kapov was escorting Tatyana Nikolaevna Rybin on a walk. He was tall, thin, silent and wan. He liked to move his cheekbone with his muscles, clenching his teeth.

She was thickset and not so young, with a yellowish cast to her skin. She wore a hurt expression on her face.

They walked along.

I. Her Walk

An awful day!

What can be more repulsive than a Parisian Sunday!

There's a breeze from the river. Maybe there's a breeze on weekdays, too, but then it's not as noticeable. On weekdays Tatyana Nikolaevna runs to and from work, she hurries and bustles about—what's the weather to her? But today, on Sunday, when she's outside for her own pleasure, so to speak, this weather gets on her nerves.

The sun is shining—unpleasantly so. It plants freckles on noses and nothing more. And the wind's blowing. So you walk along like a fool and you're supposed to be happy.

What is this habit of absolutely having to take a walk? He should at least consider her tastes a little. Why can't he understand that she'd rather go to the movies? She, of course, is a discreet person and can't just come right out with what she wants. First of all, maybe he doesn't have much money, and second, she doesn't want to make it too obvious that it's boring to be with him, that there's nothing to talk about with him, that she's altogether tired of him. And once he realizes that, then the reproaches and tragedies will certainly begin, some rusty revolver like the one Ivan Nikolaevich had will appear, and he'll wave this weapon first in front of his nose, then in front of her own. What can be worse than an hysterical man? And he's the hysterical type. He's one of those who suffers with special fervor. You have to be careful with him.

It was boring to stroll. But still it was better than sitting in a tiny room and polishing your nails for lack of anything else to do, while he smokes and lazily deals out solitaire. Oh, but why! Why all this torment?

She stopped on the bridge and looked through the railing for a long time. The water was churning and swirling.

"Let's go," he said. "Don't stare like that."

It was as if he understood something. Could he have guessed? You have to be careful. He looks somehow strained. Why did he have to fall so madly in love with her?

Well, for her part she was doing everything she could. Like right now, on a Sunday, instead of going to Varya Valikova's, where people had probably gathered (Lord! Even that would be more pleasant than this idiotic walk), she has to drag herself along, like a goat on a rope, after this innately suicidal person.

"Maybe we could stop in at a cafe?" he asks.

"No, *merci*," she answers. "I'd rather stroll."

To stop in at a cafe, that means to sit in a stuffy place reeking of tobacco smoke and beer and watch the virtuous petty bourgeois playing pinochle with their wives beside them, stupidly peeking at their cards. And all the while her gallant would conduct some leisurely conversation, totally uninteresting to her.

Maybe she should say to him outright: "I know and I believe that you love me, but look, I don't love you. Get that into your head and don't burden me with your tragedies and death."

Here they crossed the street and he took her by the arm.

"He's looking for an opportunity to touch me," she thought with disgust. "How awful this primitive passion is!"

"Maybe you'd like to go to the movies?" he suddenly asked, and she saw a strange expression on his face, not quite of supplication or of despair. He probably wants to give her pleasure and is afraid she'll agree to go. That would mean she's bored with him and there's nothing to talk about.

"No," she said. "I'll gladly walk on a little more. At the movies you can't see each other or carry on a conversation."

There! To sacrifice herself more than she's sacrificing already is impossible. And it's all out of pity and fear for this drivelling neurotic, this degenerate—to hell with him—in case he should kill himself.

They had to talk about something, though.

"Oh, look at that cute doggie run," she exclaimed, smiling full of suffering.

"Yes, he's running," he answered. "It's the natural thing for him to do."

She understood that this vapid conversation about doggies was unpleasant for him.

But you know you can't mutter about your feelings all the time. She was silently indignant. He's the most banal type. He can't even maintain the simplest conversation. How could I ever tolerate our closeness? Why couldn't I see?

"Do you remember the first time we met, at the Belikovs'?" she involuntarily asked.

A spasm ran across his face.

"Hm . . ." he answered and blushed just a bit.

"What does 'hm' mean?" she asked, annoyed. "Don't you want to talk to me?"

Frightened, he grabbed her by the hand. "What do you mean! On the contrary, I want to terribly. Dreadfully want to. Really madly want to."

What an hysterical type!

"Well, then why don't you answer when you're spoken to?"

"I couldn't think of what to answer. That is, not what to answer, but how to answer. I was confused. For Christ's sake don't think . . . Well, I was simply surprised that suddenly, right here on the bridge . . . to come out with that . . . my memory, as they say, was stirred. Darling, you're looking at me strangely, as if you don't believe me. You do know . . ."

"I know, I know, I know everything," she interrupted with irritation. "Take me home, I have a headache."

"No, something's wrong," he jumped at her. "There's something wrong here. You obviously didn't understand me correctly. You can't really doubt my feelings for you?" he asked in despair.

"No, of course not, no, I believe you, I believe you," she answered in irritation and, sighing, added, "Take me home."

At the door of her house she peered attentively into his downcast face and suddenly turned to him in despair and kissed his forehead.

"Goodbye. Come again soon," she muttered, noting with horror how he blossomed from her kiss and walked off down the street with a cheerful, lively gait.

II. His Walk

What a wonderful day! There's a light breeze from the river, and the spring sun is bright. How charming! If only I could spend the day the way I wanted to! Without any idiotic romances, sighs, and psychologies, but just chatting with Mishka Petukhov, let's say, and walking to a tavern in Saint Cloud for a bite to eat and a swig of vodka—maybe even a second and a third. To unburden my heart, to curse out those misers the Porshevichs, that swindler Boriskin, that fool Klopotova; to have everything simple, cozy and sincere.

But this peahen here has gotten herself all gussied up to go strutting along. She's incomprehensible and as boring as overcooked veal. She walks along without saying a word. And you know if you don't drop in on her on Sunday, she'll raise such hysterics that you can't disentangle yourself for a week. Or maybe nothing would happen if I didn't show? Somehow I've got to take courage and blurt it out right away. Once and for all. But will she hang herself? Yes, she's just the type. And she'd probably choose the most disgusting death, with her tongue hanging out. So you have to walk her along like an organ grinder walking his monkey.

She stopped on the bridge and began to stare at the water.

What a depressing nose she has, he thought with aversion. And why is she staring? Probably thoughts of suicide and other histrionics. Oh, why does she cling to me?

"Let's go," he said. "Don't stare like that."

What anguish! And with every step the irritation grows.

"Let's stop in at a cafe," he suggested.

She refused. Out of spite, of course. But why is she angry? Does she want me to express my love constantly? Such witches do exist!

She glanced at him quickly. Out of fright he grabbed her hand. He suggested they go to the movies. She didn't want to go. Well, to hell with her.

They walked along.

They walked along unbearably. He could just scream!

"Look at the doggie run!" she was suddenly moved to say.

Oh, you dingbat, he thought. 'The doggie run,' what sentimental claptrap! 'Doggie.' What an infant, hah, as if she never saw a dog run! A poor excuse for a person.

Her face was angry. Well, if only she wouldn't turn to cheap endearments.

"Do you remember the first time we met?"

Oh, no! Here it comes, she's getting mushy.

He was simply repulsed. He wanted to yell to the whole street: "I remember that meeting, dammit! Re-m-em-ber!" His temperature shot up. What is she blabbering about now?

"You don't want to talk to me and blah-blah-blah and blah-blah-blah..."

Well, she's started in on it. I'll calm her down as best I can. I've put a noose around my own neck! Your head hurts? Well, glory be to God. If only she doesn't lure me to her house to deal out fortune-telling cards. Why is there so much nonsense in the world? So much silly, silly nonsense!

At her door she suddenly kissed his forehead.

"Darling," he muttered, but it seems she wasn't listening. Well, let her not listen. To hell with her. Thank God people sometimes get headaches. What freedom that a head can ache, that is, freedom for the other head that doesn't.

Where to now? Well, nowhere. I'll just walk along the quay. What a charming wind! I'll have to drop in tomorrow anyway. Otherwise, who knows, she might even hang herself. Really, it's impossible to be serene for a single minute with that type. I'm a kind person, it's difficult for me. Although maybe—here's a sinful thought—maybe it wouldn't be so bad if she did . . .?

A Banal Story

Often enough it happens that a person writes two letters and seals them, mixing up the envelopes by mistake.

All sorts of amusing and unpleasant consequences could result, but since absent minded people are the ones who usually make this mistake, the scatter-brains usually manage to blunder out of their foolish situations the same way they got into them. Everyone just laughs them off. But when the misfortune befalls a solid family man, the consequences are not so amusing.

In fact, they can be tragic.

However, strange as it may seem, human error sometimes brings the offender more good than his well-thought-out and rational deeds.

The incident I wish to relate happened to just such a serious and uncommonly family-minded man. I say "uncommonly family-minded," because by virtue of his domestic inclinations (a quality quite rare in contemporary society, and therefore especially valuable), he had two complete families at once.

The first family—with which he lived—consisted of a wife, with whom he did not live, and a daughter, Linochka, young but very promising. Already she had kept her promises twice—but that has nothing to do with our story.

The second family, with which he did not live, was more complicated.

It consisted of a wife, with whom he lived, and strangely enough, the husband of this wife. There was also someone's mama and a brother. It was a large family, and intricate, demanding some attentiveness.

Our hero had to give the mama warm shawls and cards for fortune-telling. He had to give the husband cigars and lend money to the brother without any hope of repayment. And to Viktoria Orestovna, the charmer herself, he was called upon to give rings, cologne, fox stoles, and other necessities for a woman of spiritual needs.

Strictly speaking, he found no particular joy in either this family or the other. In the family where he lived, there was a suffering wife who constantly demanded compassion and respect for her grief and exhausted him with her pose of meek submission. "She's a lousy Lady Godiva," he would say about her.

Also belonging to the family where he lived was his own daughter, Linochka, who stuck her nose everywhere it didn't belong, listened in on phone conversations, stole letters, and endeavored to blackmail her sometimes forgetful father.

"Papochka! Who did you buy this pin for? For me or for Mamochka?"

"Which pin? What are you chattering about?"

"I saw the receipt."

"What receipt? What kind of nonsense is this?"

"It fell out of your vest."

Papochka blushed deeply and averted his eyes.

Then Linochka would go over to him like a soft kitten and lisp: "Papotska! Give Linotska thiwty fwancs for a dwess. Linotska is your faithful fwiend!"

There was always such a mean glint in her eyes that Papochka took fright, giving her the money.

In the family where he didn't live, everyone had his own studied pose, too.

Viktoria "loved and suffered from duplicity." Her husband, the meek and innocent Vanya, must never find out... But deceiving him was so painful for her.

"Darling! If you prefer, maybe we should just die together?"

Papochka darling would take fright and then take Viktoria out to eat.

The pose of the "innocent" Vanya was that of a madly loving husband, both trusting and magnanimous, in whom suspicion might at any moment begin to stir.

The brother's pose was: "I understand everything and therefore I forgive everything. But sometimes my moral sense is outraged. My poor sister . . ."

To put the moral sense back to sleep again, Papochka had to lend him money right away.

The mama's pose was clear and simple: "Why do they bother with all this nonsense? If he'd just fork over a heap of money, he could go to hell for all I care."

Of course, the hero of this sad affair did not perceive all the details of these poses, but he was aware of an unpleasant and uneasy atmosphere.

The atmosphere had become even more uneasy recently, ever since some artist with a guitar had taken a liking to Viktoria. He wheezed out gypsy romances and gazed at Viktoria with limpid eyes. She called him her brilliant Yurochka. Several times she made Papochka bring him along when they went out to eat, pretending to be afraid of the gossip if they were seen too often alone together.

Papochka keenly disliked this new development. Up until now he'd at least had the consolation that he had not yet been thrown out,

A Banal Story

that he enjoyed a "beautiful sin" with a married woman, and that he made a man significantly younger than himself jealous. But now, in the presence of "brilliant Yurochka" (who, incidentally, had already borrowed money from him twice), the beautiful sin lost all its spice. It became boring and trite. Still—gloomy, stubborn and business-like, he kept on visiting that chaotic house, as if he were doing his duty.

Papochka would have felt awkward in front of his other family if he'd suddenly stopped leaving the house at his usual hours. He feared the suspicious, perhaps scornful (or worse yet, joyful) glances of his wife, and the malicious allusions of Linochka.

The Christmas holidays found him in a tangle of uncertain emotions.

Viktoria was cultivating her mysteriousness and languor.

"No, I don't want to go anywhere Christmas Eve. For some reason I'm sad and anxious. Why are you so quiet, Evgeniy Pavlich? Do you hear—I don't want to go anywhere."

"Well," Papochka answered indifferently. "If you don't want to, we don't have to."

Viktoria's eyes glittered spitefully. "Did you have something in mind?"

"Yes, I thought we could go to Montmartre."

"To Montmartre," brilliant Yurochka piped up. "That's an idea! Why not? I could meet you there."

"And poor Vanya?" asked Viktoria. "I don't want him to be bored all alone."

"I'm free," announced the brother. "I could join you, too."

"And I could wear your moleskin cape," Mamenka announced unexpectedly.

"Yes, but what about poor Vanya?" Viktoria repeated stubbornly. "Evgeniy Pavlovich! I won't go without him."

"Clever," thought Evgeniy Pavlovich. "This means dragging the whole blessed family along. Am I that much of a fool?"

"Well, darling." He smiled tenderly. "If you don't want to go, then don't force yourself. I'll gladly sit at home, as in the old days."

He took his hostess's hand, kissed it, and began to say goodbye to the others.

Viktoria was roused. "I'll call you. That is, you call me tomorrow."

"If I can," Papochka replied in a genteel tone.

He liked this genteel tone very much. So much, that he immediately decided to establish it firmly in himself.

The next morning, Christmas Eve morning, his suffering wife said to him: "Don't get angry, Evgesha, but Linochka invited some people over for this evening. It will be very informal, but I felt I should tell you anyway."

"What makes you think I won't be home?" Evgeniy Pavlovich was suddenly indignant. "Who asked you to organize my life? And who are you to forbid me from staying home if I want to?"

This exchange turned out to be extraordinarily silly. The suffering wife didn't know what to say. Her role was to stand before her husband in meek reproach. But now it was *he* who was reproaching her.

She felt like a prima donna whose customary role had been stolen without warning and given to an artist of a completely different *emploie*.

"What are you saying, Evgesha?" she began to babble. "On the contrary, I'm terribly glad . . ."

"We know this terrible gladness!" Papochka growled and left to make a phone call.

He called Viktoria, of course, but her brother came to the phone.

"Tell her I'm very sorry, but I simply can't tear myself away tonight."

"What do you mean?" the brother's voice rose threateningly. "We've already gotten ready. We might have turned down hundreds of invitations! We might have spent money on this outing!"

Papochka held his breath and hung up the receiver very softly. Let the brother think that he'd left the phone long ago!

But Papochka felt uneasy.

His wife walked around the house, confused. She kept turning around cautiously, drawing her head into her shoulders as if afraid that he'd whack her on the back of the neck. She whispered about something with Linochka, who just shrugged her shoulders.

Papochka was nervous. He kept glancing at the telephone and muttering quietly, but with feeling:

> "No, into this forest of felled trees
> They'll never lure me, if you please!
> Where there once were oaks to the skies,
> Now only burnt-out stumps arise."

On the word "stumps" he imagined with revulsion Viktoria's mama in the moleskin cape.

That evening his suffering wife, having lost her role of misery once and for all, asked him to buy a can of sprats and about thirty tangerines.

A Banal Story

He sighed: "I'm already at her beck and call." But he went to the store and bought the tangerines and sprats.

On his way out, he saw a sumptuous basket displayed in the shop window. It was huge and square. In each of its corners reclined bottles of champagne with their bellies thrust out. A giant pineapple, with thyroid bumps like a sturgeon's spine, spread its green plume like a palm tree. Grapes, huge as pears, hung in heavy bunches. Pears, plump as brown-freckled women, pressed against the round, shining cheeks of ruddy apples. A stupendous basket!

And suddenly—a thought! "I'll send it to my other family, that band of gypsy swindlers. That'll be a noble gesture!"

For just a moment Papochka clearly pictured "brilliant" Yurochka's face as a repugnant, slobbering pineapple. But the beauty of the noble gesture overpowered the image of his face.

Even the monstrous price of the basket made Evgeniy Pavlovich happy. "Her brother will probably ask the messenger how much it cost. Ha! It's not the brilliant Yurochka who sent it to you. It's the noble and lordly Evgeniy Pavlovich."

Papochka took out his card and wrote Viktoria's address on it.

The salesman would not allow such an excellent customer to carry the package of tangerines and sprats himself. He seized that purchase and made Evgeniy Pavlovich write his own address on a card.

And here, in this very place, Evgeniy Pavlovich's fate took a new turn. The sickly tangerines and plebian sprats went to the swindlers, while the stupendous basket went directly to his own house, and so quickly, that it was there on the dining room table to greet him when he arrived, surrounded by the puzzled but joyful faces of his suffering wife, the mean Linochka, the maid Marya, even the cook, Anna Timofeevna (herself from a noble family).

The guests soon arrived. Kavochka Busova, Linochka's merry friend, became slightly tipsy from the champagne and squeezed Papochka's hand under the table.

Papochka was touched. "What a peach! And all from a single glass!"

He considered himself an utter fool to waste any more time and money on the boring Viktoria, who got hiccups from champagne.

"No, into this forest of felled trees . . ."

****

For a long time Viktoria remained firm, giving no sign of life.

Papochka slept well, gained weight, and cheered up. He took Kavochka to the movies.

But finally the swindlers began to stir. A letter arrived from the brother: "If you are still interested in the fate of the woman you hurt and humiliated, please be informed that her brother doesn't have a spring coat."

Papochka yawned, stretched, and said to his formerly suffering wife, "Why don't you ever order kidney soup, *ma chère*? Maybe with giblets?"

To which the former sufferer, having lost her role entirely, answered distractedly, indifferently: "All right, all right, if I get the chance, and I don't forget."

A Psychological Fact

It seems to me I'm a ruined man.

I'm sure nothing can help me—not pills, not even a holiday in the South.

I'm at the end of my tether. I've been drinking for four days, and I'm not a drinker, you know. Ordinarily I conduct myself like a gentleman and I never scandalize—but at this point I can't vouch for my behavior.

How did this happen, and why? It's as if I lost control of myself.

What kind of man am I?

I'll take a look at myself from the outside.

Am I normal? Of course I'm normal! Even more than normal—I've always controlled myself too well. If I happened to be insulted, I never made a scene. I just smiled in response like the purest of gentlemen.

I'm kind. For example, I gave Penin fifteen francs, knowing he'd never repay me, and I'll never reproach him for it.

I'm not jealous. If someone is happy—to hell with him, let him be happy, I don't give a damn.

I love to read. I'm intellectually developed. I got *Niva** for 1892 and read it with enthusiasm.

My outward appearance is pleasant. My face is full and serene.

I have a job.

In short, I'm a man.

So what happened to me? Why am I crowing like a rooster and soaking up vodka like a sponge? It will pass, of course, but what exactly occurred? I really shouldn't be telling anyone, you know. It's a psychological affair, which has shaken me up for four days now. Although once you think about it and begin talking about it, my trouble doesn't seem like such a tragedy after all. But how did I ever get into this condition? Where did such a psychological fact arise? . . . .

Let's talk calmly about *her* now. Completely calmly. And we'll cast an outsider's glance upon her, too.

At first glance she is, above all, terribly tall. As they used to say in Russia, "You could hang a cow on a person like that." No doubt this saying is full of folk wisdom, but when did anyone ever have the opportunity to hang a cow? When are they hung? . . . . But enough! I don't want to waste time on such difficult and confusing reflections.

---

*Niva was a popular, illustrated weekly of the late nineteenth century—not a serious intellectual journal. (Trans.)

So, she's tall and ungainly. Her arms dangle at her sides. Her legs splay out. They're amazing legs—the higher up they go, the thinner they get.

She never laughs. Strange to say, I established this fact only now, towards the end of our existence together. It wasn't that I didn't notice earlier (how could one *not* notice that!), but somehow I just didn't comprehend.

Next I must mention that she's not good-looking. And it's not just a matter of my own personal taste. She's not good-looking to anyone's taste. Her face looks permanently pained and discontented.

But the main thing is that she's a fool. You certainly can't debate that point. It's obvious and it's definite. But just imagine! I didn't notice it right away. It certainly seems as though her silliness should have hit me smack between the eyes, but for some reason it didn't yield to my instant definition. Not anticipating any development in our relationship, I didn't dwell on it.

But let's get to the story-telling.

I met her at the Efimovs' (they're always throwing curves at me!). As soon as she arrived, she asked what time it was. Told it was ten o'clock, she answered: "That means I can sit with you for exactly half an hour, because I must be in a certain place at exactly eight-thirty."

At this point Efimov laughed and said there really was no use hurrying, because eight-thirty had passed an hour and a half ago.

In a hurt tone she replied that there was a big difference between being two hours late or three.

Efimov laughed again. "That means you believe it's more convenient to be five minutes late for a train than half an hour?"

She was surprised: "Of course!"

I didn't yet know she was a fool and thought she was merely joking.

Then it turned out I had to escort her home.

On the way I learned that her name was Raisa Konstantinovna, that her husband was a chauffeur, and that she worked in a restaurant.

"My family life is ideal," she said. "My husband is a night chauffeur. When I get home, he's already gone, and by the time he returns, I'm gone. Never any quarrels. We live soul to soul."

She's being witty, I thought. But no, her face was serious. She said what she was thinking.

In order to keep the conversation going, I asked if she liked the movies. She answered by saying, "Fine. How about Thursday?"

Well, what could I do? I couldn't tell her that I hadn't really meant to invite her. That would have been rude.

So on Thursday I stopped by to pick her up. And it all started with that evening.

Strange things happen in this world, you know!

For example, I was leading her along, holding her hand.

"You are so charming," I said. (One has to say *something*, after all.)

"I guessed that long ago," she replied.

"Guessed what?" I asked, surprised.

"That you love me."

She let it fall just like that. I stopped dead in my tracks.

"Who?" I said. "That is, whom? What did you say?"

She talked to me as if from the heights of Olympia: "No need to feel so flustered! You're not the first, you won't be the last, and besides, love is a completely natural phenomenon."

My eyes goggled; I was dumbstruck. And I still didn't realize what a fool she was!

Meanwhile, she continued to dwell on her own strange thoughts, developing them in the most unexpected direction. And she was speaking in all seriousness.

"We won't tell my husband anything for now," she said. "Maybe we can later on, once your fateful emotions have taken a more definite shape."

I grabbed her with both hands. "Exactly! Exactly! We won't say anything!"

"I will be an unattainable dream for you. I'll mend your underwear, I'll read poetry with you. Do you like cheese pancakes? I'll make cheese pancakes for you sometime. Our intimacy should be like a golden dream."

All I could repeat was, "Yes, a dream! Exactly!"

To be honest, this idea of hers about darning did spark a smile in me. I'm a solitary man, disorderly, and a female like that, who instantly displays feminine solicitude, is a great rarity in our times. Of course, I found her response to my compliment somewhat extreme, but since it called forth such remarkable results—like putting my wardrobe in order—I could only feel glad and thankful. I didn't like her, of course, but (again some folk wisdom!) you can't drink water from a face, let alone from a body.

When we said goodbye I kissed her hands. And later, during the night, thinking over the whole adventure, I even smiled to myself. In my solitary life I can only welcome the appearance of such a useful woman. Also I remembered the cheese pancakes. And you know, it didn't seem too bad. Not too bad at all.

Once I had decided that things weren't so bad, I calmed down.

All About Love

The next day I came home from work, opened the door, and found her sitting in my room. She'd brought me some rusks.

"I've thought things over and decided," she said. "You can use the familiar form of address with me."

"Please! I'm not worthy of it!" I protested.

"I permit you to," she said.

The hell with that! I really didn't want to! So I stood firm. "I'm not worthy of it and that's that."

But she just kept on talking—and about the strangest things.

"I know you're suffering," she said. "But suffering enobles. You must look at me as a higher being, as your unattainable ideal. We don't need vulgar passions—we're not cannibals, after all. A poet once said: 'Only the morning of love is good.' . . . . Here, I brought you some rusks. Of course, the rusks they have here don't compare with those they make in Chuevo, back in Russia. They make such garbage here! They have no idea . . .! Do you know, more than anything in you I value the fact that you're Russian. The French, you know, are utterly incapable of lofty feelings. If a Frenchman does marry, it's only for two years. Then comes betrayal and divorce."

"What are you talking about? Where did you get that idea? I happen to know many respectable married couples among the French."

"Well, they're the exceptions. If they don't get divorced, it's only because they like to save money together. Do they really have any spiritual needs? Everything about them is unnatural. Their flowers aren't natural, their cucumbers are as big as logs, and they don't understand dill at all. And wine! You certainly can't get natural wine here for any price. Everything is imitation."

"What are you saying!" I cried out. "France is renowned throughout the world for its wine. The best wine in the world is made in France."

"How naive you are! It's all imitation," she insisted.

"Where did you get that idea?" I spluttered.

"A certain man explained it all to me."

"A Frenchman?"

"Of course not!" she said indignantly. "A Russian."

"How does he know?"

"He just knows," she answered stubbornly.

"Does he work for winegrowers or something?"

"Of course not! He lives near us in Vaugirard."

"Then how can he possibly judge?" I cried in exasperation.

"Why shouldn't he? He's lived in Paris four years. He observes things. It's not as easy for others to avert their eyes as it is for you."

I realized that I was beginning to tremble from irritation. However, I controlled myself and stated in the most genteel tone: "Well, this Russian of yours is simply an idiot."

"Well! If it pleases you to degrade your own blood..."

"I don't have to degrade him. He's already an idiot!"

"Well, you can just go and kiss your Frenchmen! You probably like their beef, too. But just tell me where their fillets are? Where is their rump? Can their beef ever compare to ours? Their steers don't even have the parts ours have! We have Circassian steers. But they don't even have an inkling of what Circassian beef is."

I didn't understand exactly what was going on, but for some reason it made me terribly angry. I'm not a Frenchman, so there was nothing for me to be insulted about—especially not beef—but still I felt upset.

"Excuse me, Raisa Konstantinovna," I said, "but I will not permit you to talk this way about the country which gives us refuge. I consider it ugly and ungrateful on your part."

She began to scream at me: "Stand up for them! Go ahead and stand up for them! Maybe you even like the fact that there's no sour cream here? Don't be embarrassed, please, tell the truth. Do you like it? Are you ready to applaud the fact that there isn't a dollop of sour cream in all of France? Are you glad of the chance to trample on dear Russia?"

Her mouth twisted, her face turned pale. She was so tall and repulsive. "You're trampling, trampling on Russia!" she cried.

What came over me, I myself don't know. I grabbed her by the shoulders and began to yell in a goat-like voice: "Get out of here, you fool!"

I yelled so loudly that the neighbors knocked on the wall. I was utterly shaken. On the stairway she screamed something about Russia again. I didn't listen. I trampled her rusks with my feet. I did well to, because if I had run after her instead, I would have finished her off for good. At that instant there was a killer within me.

So I was only a hair away from the guillotine. Because how do you explain a Russian fool to a French jury?

They wouldn't understand it. That's one thing the French really cannot manage.

It's just not in their nature.

The Gentleman

One remarkable day they met, completely by chance, while transferring at the Trocadero metro station. She was changing for Passy, he was taking *direction Saint Cloud*. Right in the corridor, at the turnstyle that whacks dawdlers in the stomach, they met.

Out of surprise she dropped her purse, and he cried: "Varya!" Startled by his own cry, he clutched his head with both hands. Then they threw themselves at each other.

She (so it will be clear why he was so agitated) was very pretty, with a pug nose. She looked out at God's world with merry, somewhat heavy-lidded eyes through ringlets of blonde hair which tumbled down onto her brows. She was dressed coquettishly, painstakingly. All of her garments were embroidered with cock's combs and cockerels.

He (so it will be clear why she dropped her purse) was a tall, elegant gentleman with a part beginning right at the bridge of his nose—so that even under a hat it was hard to hide its source. Necktie, handerchief, socks—everything matched. Only the expression on his face spoiled things a bit—it showed a cross between confusion and fright. However, that's a mere trifle.

They threw themselves at each other and grabbed hands.

"Are you glad you ran into me?" the woman began to babble. "Really? Really glad?"

"Madly! Madly! I... I love you!" he exclaimed and stepped back to clutch his head again. "My God, what am I doing! For God's sake, forgive me! An unexpected meeting... I lost my head! I should never have dared! Forget it! Forgive me! Varvara Petrovna!"

"No, no! You called me Varya! Call me Varya always... I love you."

"O-o-o!" he began to moan. "You love me? That means we're doomed!"

Out of agitation he began to lisp. He took off his hat and mopped his short forehead.

"Everything is doomed," he continued. "We must never meet again!"

"Why not?" Varya was surprised.

"I am a gentleman and I must be concerned with your reputation and your safety. What if your husband notices something? What if he insults you with his suspicion? What would happen to me

All About Love

then—a duel? A bullet in my forehead? How dreadful that would be!"

"Wait a minute," said Varya. "Let's sit down on the bench and talk."

He followed her with gestures of limitless despair and sat down next to her.

"What if people see us here?"

"What if they do?" Varya was surprised. "I ran into Pastor Lukin here yesterday and we chatted for an hour and a half. What business is it of anyone's?"

"That's true," he agreed tragically. "But you're forgetting that he's not in love with you, nor you with him. As for us... The whole secret of our relationship will come to the surface. And what then—a bullet in my forehead?"

"Oh, what nonsense! Vasily Dmitrich! Darling! We're just losing time over nothing. Tell me again that you love me. When did you first fall in love with me?"

He looked around on all sides.

"On a Thursday. I fell in love with you on a Thursday. A month ago, at dinner at Madame Compote's. You reached your hand out for a roll and I was somehow struck by your exquisite gesture. I became so agitated that I grabbed the salt cellar and sprinkled salt into my wine. Everyone exclaimed: 'What are you doing?' But I didn't lose my head. 'I always drink wine like this,' I said. Didn't I get out of that one cleverly? The trouble is that now, whenever I dine or lunch somewhere with common acquaintances, I always have to sprinkle salt into my wine. There's no way around it. Otherwise they might guess!"

"How wonderful you are," sighed Varya. "Vasya, darling!"

"Wait a minute!" Vasya interrupted her. "What do you call your husband?"

"What? Misha, of course."

"Well then, I greatly implore you: call me Misha, too. Then you will never slip up. So many misfortunes occur just because of a name. Imagine—your husband kisses you, and you're dreaming about me just then. You involuntarily whisper my name. 'Vasya, Vasya, again!' Or something like that. And he just stops dead. 'What's with this Vasya? Why Vasya? Which one of our friends is Vasya? Aha! Kurikov! I suspected it long ago!' and it will go on and on. And what will be the end of it—a bullet in my forehead? But if you get used to calling me Misha (you know, I could in fact have been a Misha—everything depends upon one's parents' whim), if you get used to calling me Misha, you will be saved. He kisses you, and you're dreaming about me and whispering about me—about *me*, you

The Gentleman

understand—'Misha, Misha.' And that fool husband of yours will be happy and serene. Or in your sleep, for example. In your sleep you might dream about me, and you could babble my name. And your husband is right there! He wakes up to look at the clock, and he listens and listens. 'Vasya? What's this Vasya bit? Vasya?' Well, and it will go on and on. I am a gentleman. I—well, what? I should shoot a bullet into my own forehead?"

"How serious everything is for you!" Varya muttered with displeasure. "No one else is like that. Lovers always call each other by name and no problems ever arise from it, on the contrary—only pleasure."

"My God, how inexperienced you are! Half of all divorces are based on these Vasinkas and Petinkas. And why? What for? If it's so easy to avoid?"

"Aren't *you* afraid of slipping up? You know, you called me Varya today. What if you call me that again?"

"Well, I certainly shan't call you that now. It happened because our relationship was still unclear to us. But now, when I as a gentleman must be on guard and must think about you, only you, dear (forgive me for calling you dear, that's also a foolish imprudence), I shall no longer risk entangling you in a sticky situation."

"What will you call me, then, I'm curious to know? After all, you're not married. Hm?"

"I live alone, that is, I live with my mama. I could call you 'Mama,' of course. It's like a habit. If a man lives with his mama, he can't help but make a slip in speaking from time to time. No, I won't risk a thing if I call you 'Mama, dear.' If someone hears, he'll just think, 'That man is remembering his mama,' and everything will seem completely natural."

"This is really... the devil knows what! What kind of mama am I to you? Next you'll begin to honor me with 'Granny.' It's silly and it's impolite."

"O dear—that is, Varvara Petrovna. I'm doing all this only out of delicacy, you know."

"Will you be at Doctor Fogelblat's anniversary party tomorrow? I secretly asked the toastmaster to seat us next to each other. My husband will be sitting with the committee, so we can chat a little. I'm terribly glad that I thought of..."

"What have you done!" exclaimed Vasya. "There's no way I can go to the banquet now! Of course, if we had our former, purely friendly relationship, it would be lovely to go. But now—it's unthinkable! How exasperating! I already paid my money, and now I can't go. But what about this? I'll call the toastmaster myself and, as

All About Love

if I didn't know anything, I'll tell him he absolutely has to seat me next to, let's say, Doctor Sitsina. Yes. Good idea?"

"And if he says that I asked him to seat you next to me?"

"In that case I'll just pretend that I've forgotten who you are. 'Which Varvara Petrovna is that?' I'll ask. 'The fat one who makes up to everyone?' You understand, I'll treat you negatively on purpose. That is, not *you* exactly, but as though I've confused you with someone else. 'She's so dirty and pimply,' I'll say. You understand? So that it's clear that I don't even know whom we're talking about."

"Excuse me, but that's absolutely ridiculous," Varya flared up. "Toastmaster Penkin has seen you at my house so many times, how can he possibly believe that you suddenly don't know me?"

"I'll speak so badly of you that he'll have to believe it. I'll say something exceptionally vulgar. Don't worry, I'll be able to, I won't be at a loss."

"But I don't want you to say all kinds of foul things about me!"

"Darling! That is, Varvara Petrovna, that is, Granny—whatever your name is! I'm all mixed up. I wanted to begin getting used to it and already I'm mixed up. Mama dear! You know this is all for you, for you alone. Do you really think I enjoy combining your name with various nasty adjectives? Do you think it's not painful for me? But there's nothing I can do about it. It's absolutely necessary. Tomorrow I shall sit next to the lady doctor. Then I'll cast careless glances at the other guests, nod my head condescendingly towards you, and let a word drop. You understand? Just let a word drop, speak condescendingly, through my teeth. Very condescendingly. I'll nod and squeeze out through my teeth: 'Ugh, so that little fool is here.' And then the doctor not only will *not* believe in our intimacy, she'll even argue the others out of it, should anyone begin to suspect. Of course, this is very difficult for me, but what I won't do for my lady! I'm a knight. A gentleman. I will not give you over to insult. And if a conversation about you does start up among the guests, you can rest assured I'll paint such a picture of you that no one would even dream of thinking that I like you. I'll ridicule everything, your dress, your manners, your appearance. 'Ha-ha,' I'll say, 'that Varka has a nose like a ski jump. See how she struts along.' Or: 'So she's planning a party? With her manners she should be milking cows instead of receiving guests.' I'll certainly think of something. 'She imagines she can be charming,' I'll say. 'Ha-ha!' In a word, Mama, you can rest assured. I'll defend your honor. It will be painful for me, of course. And of course it's better that I don't frequent your house anymore. Oh, and then I'll say, '*I* wasn't the one who saw her serving cheap cookies from Uniprix at fifty kopecks a pound. But that's what her snub-nosed parties are always like.' I'll think something up, that's for sure. But my God, how difficult and painful all of this is! What? What? I can't understand what you're saying. M-Mama?"

"Go to hell! That's what I'm saying!" cried Varya, jumping up from the bench. "Beat it to the devil, you blithering idiot! And don't you dare come after me, you repulsive person!"

She turned quickly and ran down the stairs.

"Va... that is, Ma..." Vasya mumbled in horror. "What's happening? Why so suddenly, in the very heat of my sacrificial love? Maybe she saw one of our acquaintances and acted out a scene? That's clever, if that's what she did. Very clever. Remarkably so. If someone saw us, he'll immediately think: 'Aha, she doesn't like that gentleman at all.' And then if he sees us together in society, he'll no longer be dangerous to us. Yes, that was very smart on her part. Although it must have been painful for her to speak so crudely to such a beloved person. A gentleman. But what else could she do?"

Vasya stuck his hands in his pockets and whistling carefreely, so that no one would suspect anything, he began to descend the staircase.

"I love and I am loved," he thought. "Now that's true happiness. Only we must be careful. Otherwise what? A bullet in my forehead?"

The Wonder of Spring

At Doctor Luvier's sanatorium, the Easter holiday was celebrated with roast chicken and vol-au-vents filled with ham.

After breakfast the patients dressed up and began to wait for their visitors. Towards evening they were already irritable from the day's excitement and from the unaccustomed refreshments, which their visitors brought them on the sly. They buzzed angrily for the attendants, playing tricks with their room numbers. The nurses rushed about with hot camomile tea and hot-water bottles, and even the normally soothing voice of the doctor changed to a grumble.

"Why do they torment me with their love!" complained the Spanish woman in number five with an imaginary disease of the liver. "Why all these bouquets, why all this candy? After all, don't they know I'm dying? Call the doctor, let him give me poison to end my torment."

In number ten Madame Calieux flung a glass at her meek and slow-witted nurse, Marie. She was irritated by the Spanish woman's howls. Strictly speaking, Madame Calieux wasn't sick, either. She had simply fled domestic chaos to the sanitorium. No one ever visited her because she couldn't stand the sight of anyone, particularly her husband and children.

"Don't be grumpy!" Marie pleaded. "Be a good girl and eat some soup, so you'll get well sooner and can go home, where your poor husband misses his little wife, and your children cry for their mamochka."

Madame Calieux thought of her husband, that bald bastard who kept an actress from the Revue at her expense; she remembered her son, who forged her signature on promissory notes; and her daughter, who had run off with a pot-bellied banker. Madame Calieux hurled herself at the meek Marie.

But more than anyone else, Liza, the meek and timid Russian nurse, had the roughest time that evening. Her patient, a robust Greek general, had nibbled at some Strasbourg pâté, and excited by the taste, he and his wife began cursing each other. Handing him pâté, his wife told him he was a lop-eared fool and a faker, and for the money he was wasting on treatment, she could have gone to Monte Carlo.

The General howled that he was dying and demanded morphine.

Liza calmed him down as best she could, but he still threatened her with his fist. "You're just an old maid! A hopeless old maid! I know how you think—peace and quiet is more important than life itself. But here I am full of strength, and I'm doomed to die."

Why he was doomed to die, he himself did not know. Liza didn't know either, and turning away, she began to cry. These tears worked magic on him. He cheered up at once, forgetting about the morphine and asking for castor oil instead.

The General had a peculiar type of neurosis: at the sight of others' misfortune, his melancholy was instantaneously transformed into the best of moods. When one day, in his presence, the maid fell down the stairs and broke her leg, he whistled cheerfully all day long, and even made plans to organize a hospital play.

Yes, there are strange illnesses in this world . . .

That night Liza did not go to bed until very late. Sighing, she gathered all her old postcards with Bulgarian views, which were written all over in Russian script. Then she took down her photograph of the bald, bearded gentleman and gazed at it questioningly for a long time.

****

The next morning, after tending to her patients, Liza went downstairs.

The fat, meek Marie was hurriedly finishing her coffee. "I'm off to the station," she announced. "I have a package to pick up."

Liza followed her out onto the porch. "Maybe I'll come along with you," she said, shivering slightly from the fresh spring air.

"Better throw something on then—you'll catch cold," said Marie.

"No, the air feels good this way."

Easter was early that year. The trees bathed their rosy, sap-rich twigs in the clear, cold sky. The lawn bristled with last year's sparse, dry grass like an old brush. The clouds curled, as in a picture from a children's book. Everything was so new and fragile that no one was sure whether it would last and grow into real Spring or just flash with promise before declining again into Winter.

The bright sky, the budding flowers, and the fact that she had light-headedly run outside in just her dress, as in her younger days— all this suddenly hit Liza right in the heart, like spring wine. Her yellow face took on color, the wrinkles smoothed around her mouth, full of suffering, and her withered lips smiled senselessly, happily.

"I always feel like this! Everything, everything is fine with me!" she cried in a ringing voice, tossing her head.

The Wonder of Spring

Marie glanced at her with surprise. She had been working at the sanatorium all of two months and barely knew Liza.

"You Russians are very peculiar," she said. "That's why everyone falls in love with you."

Liza began to laugh capriciously and cheerfully. "Yes, they *do* fall in love with us, but not with all of us, by far."

There was something significant in her tone of voice, though it was purely unintentional, since she was not alluding to herself at all.

The spring air was intoxicating and cheering. Logs lay fallen along the side of the road, and Liza suddenly hopped up onto a thick, fallen lime tree and, balancing with her hands, ran along its length before leaping off.

"How nimble you are!" exclaimed Marie. "Like a young thing!"

Liza turned around. Her face was flushed, and her hair had tumbled out from under her nurse's cap.

The mailman, pasing by, called out: "Bravo! Bravo!"

Liza threw him a cunning glance.

Marie was as much delighted as surprised. "Oh, what a naughty girl you are! I always thought you were so quiet, but you're really an imp. All the patients must be crazy about you!"

"All of them? I'm not so sure!" Liza smiled coquettishly. "Mailman! Wait a minute. Don't you have a letter for Mademoiselle Lise Kornoff?"

The mailman, looking at her with sparkling eyes, twirling his moustache, began to dig in his bag.

"He's certainly pleased to have you chat with him," Marie whispered joyfully.

"Mademoiselle Kor-noff. Right?" asked the mailman, handing Liza a postcard.

Liza glanced at the pink rabbit carrying a blue egg with the golden letters X.B.* in its paws. She could see that the stamp was Bulgarian, but she couldn't read the writing without her glasses. That didn't matter. All that mattered was that after almost a three-month silence she had received a greeting. She was not forgotten; everything she had begun to consider dead and lost forever still lived and promised and beckoned her.

She slipped the card into her apron pocket and smiled cheerfully. When she raised her eyes, she saw right before her a young cherry tree, as if in riotous rapture, burst out in a hymn of white flowers. The tree was small and delicate, but it sent joy right to the sky, to the sun, to the heart.

---

*The Cyrillic letters "X.B." stand for "Christ is Risen." They are traditionally printed on Easter eggs. (Trans.)

"From *him?*" asked Marie, indicating with her glance the postcard sticking out of Liza's pocket.

Liza laughed and waved her hand. "It's an old story! He just can't understand that my freedom is dearer to me than anything else. We worked together in a hospital. He's a doctor. He was supposed to come to France, but he was delayed, and of course he's in despair."

"And you?" asked Marie.

"Me?" Liza shrugged her shoulders and laughed. "I, my dear, love my freedom."

And with a wide smile, revealing her long yellow teeth, she sang out of tune:

> "L'amour est un enfant de Bohème
> Qui n'a jamais, jamais connu de loi..."

"That's from *Carmen*," she added.

"How amazing you are! And tell me, this Greek general of yours—he's not indifferent to you, either?"

Liza shrugged her shoulders scornfully. "Do you really think I'd pay attention to the sentiments of such an insignificant boor?"

"An astounding woman," thought the goodnatured Marie. "She's not beautiful and she's not young, but she sure can drive them mad! Oh men, men, who can understand what you need?"

Liza ran with a bold and quick step she had never before known in herself. She laughed and was surprised that up until now she hadn't realized that life was so easy and wonderful.

They returned to the sanatorium a little tired. The maid called to Liza: "Better run up to your general right away. He's swearing so much he's simply out of control."

Liza desperately wanted to run to her room for her glasses, finally to learn what wonderful news the pink rabbit would bring her. But she did not dare linger, so she went to room number nine, stuffy and smoke-filled, where the angry man with the puffy face swore at her, calling her an old witch, a toad, and a parasite.

The blinds in the room were lowered. The sky beyond them had already died. Later they admitted a new patient, then a professor... But by then Liza was no longer smiling. She just quietly touched the pocket where the postcard lay and secretly, delightedly, sighed. The whole sky, the whole wonder of spring was now here, contained in this small piece of fine cardboard.

Only late in the evening, after dinner, could she run up the stairs to her room and bolt the door. Only then could she blissfully sigh: "Finally!"

She put on her glasses and sat down in the armchair so that she could afterwards dream for a long, long time . . .

The dear familiar handwriting . . . And so much was written! Obviously, it's not possible to forget me so soon . . .

"Dear Lizaveta Petrovna," said the familiar writing. "Forgive me for my long silence. The reasons for it are important. Don't be surprised at my news: in my old age I have married, and a young thing at that. But once you meet my wife, you'll understand me and won't condemn me, she is that charming. She knows you by my stories and loves you already.

Yours very truly,
N. Oblukov
P.S. Her name is Lyubov Aleksandrovna. N.O."

The Dear Departed

It all began when Balavin met Sorokin at the metro station and blurted out the news of the sudden death of Murashev.

Sorokin was upset. "What? It can't be! How? When? Who told you?"

"A friend just told me at the Trocadero transfer," Balavin explained. "Murashev suddenly took sick this morning, they brought him to the hospital, and he died."

"How dreadful! Two days ago he was alive and well."

"What is there to be surprised about?" Balavin mused. "He was probably alive two minutes before his death."

"Wait a minute," Sorokin interrupted him. "Have they told his wife yet?"

"No, she's away somewhere. It seems he himself didn't know her address—she hadn't managed to write to him yet. So they told me, at least."

"Well, let's just suppose I know her address. Completely by chance. From Petrusha Netovo. Now this is between you and me: Petrusha is with her in Juan-les-Pins."

"Really? So she's an interesting little lady?"

"So-so. But of course as a gentleman, you won't breathe a word of this to anyone, I trust."

"What do you take me for? But listen, since you're in on everything, why don't you send her a telegram? Otherwise—just think—a scandal might break. Maybe she doesn't read the papers. She'll carry on her happy little affair, and by the time she finds out she's a widow, her husband will have been a week underground. And maybe your Petrusha is less disposed to run after a woman who's not tied down."

"Hm," said Sorokin. "I see there's some sense to your thinking. Maybe I should take the sad duty upon myself. I'll send a telegram. Although I'm terribly busy today. I really should drop in at Murashev's apartment."

"There's probably no one there. He died in the hospital."

"Well, so much the better. Goodbye. I'll see you at the funeral. That's life for you: you live and live, and then suddenly you're dead."

Sorokin came up out of the metro in a troubled state, continuing to reflect on the pitiful human fate.

"At least the same dirty trick is played on everyone alike. What if it happened only to me! That would be dreadfully unpleasant. But poor Natasha Murasheva! Azure sea, loving Petrusha, aperitifs before dinner . . . She probably ordered a lot of dresses and fancy little hats, and suddenly—poof! A widow. Black crepe. Petrusha doesn't care for sorrow. Drying the tears of widows and orphans— that's not his cup of tea.

"Pardon, monsieur!"

This pardon did not concern Petrusha and widows, but a gentleman into whose side Sorokin had poked an elbow in his distraction. The victim turned around. He turned out to be not just any monsieur, but Sergei Petrovich Levashov.

"Oh, hello!" cried Sergei Petrovich. "Why are you so glum?"

"Me? I'm all right," Sorokin replied. "But poor Murashev. Did you hear? He died very suddenly this morning."

"What!" exclaimed Levashov. "Jesus! Four days ago . . . yes, yes, on Friday he dropped in on me on business. You don't know—it wasn't suicide, was it?"

"No, I don't think so."

"His business affairs were very disorganized, it seems. I know he needed money urgently."

"I don't know, I didn't hear the details. Anything can happen. And now there's some kind of suicide epidemic. But I'm in a terrible hurry. Goodbye."

Sorokin ran to the telegraph office.

"My God!" he thought. "Was it really suicide? He seemed to be such a calm, pleasant man. It's a shame that I never paid any attention to him. I hovered around his foolish wife Natasha instead. What a friend I may have lost in him! And I snickered when Natasha drove off with Petrusha to carry on a love affair. Poor, poor Murashev! Maybe if I had gone up to him in a friendly way, affectionately, I could have talked him out of such a dreadful step. I would have said: 'Dear friend, life is marvellous, to hell with everything!' I would have gently said: 'Let your fool wife go to the devil.' Such an affectionate word uttered in time can resurrect and return one to life. And now he's gone. Gone into non-existence."

At the post office Sorokin ruined four telegraph blanks. First he wanted to compose a cautious telegram, then a business-like one. Finally he decided to take revenge on the good-for-nothing wife.

The final version of the telegram read like this:

"*Venez vite stop votre malheureux mari suicidé stop horreur*
Sorokine."

Sorokin thought it would probably be more conscientious to telegraph only that Murashev had died, since suicide wasn't established yet, but then he decided it would be more painful for her this way. He was fuming.

Meanwhile, Levashov, gloomily hanging his head, was on his way home.

"It's terrible," he thought. "Still, I hope it wasn't suicide. How could I have known that his situation was so desperate? Let's assume I *had* agreed to give him that trifling four thousand—that obviously wouldn't have saved him if his situation was already so far gone. A mere palliative. A short respite, and then what? Then you either hand it out once more, or it's a question of suicide all over again. No, gentlemen, it's impossible that way. I'm not the one who's obligated, in fact... But on the other hand, if I *had* given him the money, maybe he would have gotten himself out of this mess. I should have given it to him. He pretended that my refusal didn't particularly grieve him, but now I see what kind of escape he had in mind. I should have given it to him. Now, of course, you can't go back and undo what's done. It's hard. Very hard. But how could I have known? If I'd known, then of course..."

****

Sea, sun, jazz, strapless evening gowns, suntans in shades of red, brown and olive.

But Natasha Murasheva wasn't up to it. Not up to jazz and not up to getting a tan. She sat on her balcony staring dully at the crumpled scrap of blue paper with white strips pasted on it. On the white strips a heartless apparatus had typed out cruel lines, composed by the avenger Sorokin.

Murasheva had a red nose and eyes to match. She was very grieved. She had already cried twice. Especially since for the past two days she had been thinking about her husband with affection. Because she'd been thinking about Petrusha Netovo without affection.

Petrusha Netovo had not turned out to be up to snuff. She had told him four times that her husband was late with the money he was to send, but Petrusha, as they say, only raised his eyebrows. The last time she even tried a certain ploy: she didn't eat anything for breakfast (even though it was lobster *à l'américaine* which she adored). But instead of becoming concerned and enabling her to start talking about her husband and the money, Petrusha only said in passing: "Aren't you hungry? Are you trying to lose weight?"

What an idiot! How could she compare him to Misha? Misha was at least solicitous. And she'd traded him for such a turkey! Poor Misha! He hadn't even let on that her departure was unpleasant for him. But then he must have guessed or else someone had opened his eyes. And now, without spite, without reproach, proudly and beautifully, he had departed from life. But maybe he was still alive? Dangerously wounded, but alive? She would nurse him, and their whole life together, their whole life . . .

There was a knock at the door and Petrusha came in.

"What happened?"

She looked at him and said with hatred: "My husband discovered everything and killed himself."

Petrusha whistled quietly and lowered himself onto a chair. "What now?"

"I'm leaving on the evening train."

Petrusha whistled again.

"Go away!" screamed Murasheva, and she began to cry loudly.

****

After sending off the telegram, Sorokin headed right home. He still had some business to attend to, but he was so distressed that he decided to forego his errands and await his clients at home.

As he sat and waited, he thought about death and tormented himself about Murashev.

After finishing his business and seeing his visitors out, Sorokin was all ready to go to Murashev's apartment to question the concierge about details, when suddenly the telephone brought him Balavin's voice, that same voice which had earlier reported the terrible news.

"*Mon ami*! An idiotic mistake! It's not Murashev who died, but Paryshev. He's also a friend of mine. Murashev is alive and well and just dropped in to borrow some money."

"Well, you didn't give him any, I hope? How ridiculous this is!" Sorokin interrupted him angrily. "Why do you get things mixed up and confuse people? And here I sent a telegram. Poor Natasha will probably go out of her mind. I'd better send another one right away. Oh, how ridiculous this is!"

He began to feel sorry for Natasha. A young woman who broke free for the first time in her life. It's understandable. This Murashev is depression personified. Most likely he'd never shoot himself, but given a chance, he'd no doubt shoot her. Sorokin decided he'd better phone Levashov, who had seemed quite upset.

****

After talking to Sorokin, Levashov began to laugh at himself: "No, people like that don't shoot themselves. He'll probably come running ten times more to beg money from me. I did well not to give him any. You lend money once and then you're never rid of 'em, and besides, it's not my fault if they can't organize their business. If he comes again, I won't even see him and that's that."

****

Petrusha Netovo gloomily packed his things into a suitcase. He didn't want to remain alone in Juan-les-Pins.

"This is all so silly. Because of such nonsense a good man died. If she hadn't clung to me he could have been my friend. In any case, he's the more interesting of the two. In a different way, of course, but more interesting all the same. And why did we have to take this trip? We could have stayed in Paris. The poor man. To die like that for nothing. And I didn't even notice that he knew. How he could hide his grief! A proud and beautiful soul! Oh, if only I could cry, it would be easier for me!"

'Petrusha! Petrusha!" cried Natasha, running into his room. "Petrusha! Hurray! They mixed everything up. Here's the telegram. My idiot husband is very much alive. Here, read it: "Mistake stop Murashev alive and well stop greetings to Petrusha I kiss your hands Your Sorokin."

"I'm so glad! 'I kiss your hands.' That means everything is okay. Still, it's good that he's alive. I don't love him, of course, because I'm all yours, but these tragedies are so unpleasant! Now give me a kiss and let's run to the Casino."

So Petrusha kissed her and off they ran to the Casino.

A Woman's Lot

Margarita Nikolaevna's appearance was what is called "interesting." One could study her for hours and still not know the first thing about her.

For example, what was her coloring? Her hair was auburn in the curls, yellow at the temples, red on the top, and cherry at the back of her head. Where was the true color? Where could you look with confidence? Where with indulgence for feminine weakness? Where with censure? Delight?

Her brows were thin, black, hairless threads, like a freak of pigmentation. Her lashes were blue. Nostrils lilac. Orange lips. Porcelain teeth, bluish with gold.

And all of this chaos and panoply of colors was reflected in the wise expression of her dull grey eyes. Her eyes were fifty-four years old.

Margarita Nikolaevna was reputed to be a clever woman. People came to her for advice at emotionally difficult moments. Women only. But at financially difficult moments they didn't come. That was only logical: since she was clever, it followed that she wouldn't give any money away.

Margarita Nikolaevna would sit down on the couch with her back to the light. She would seat the emotionally overwrought lady facing the window—so that not only her psychical, but also her physical secrets would more readily emerge. Then she began her questioning.

Sometimes, after a two-hour conversation, her advice was utterly simple and short: "To hell with him, and that's all there is to it."

"What? What do you mean to hell with him?" the confused woman would cry. "You forget that other time when he behaved like a moonstruck fool—he took me out to eat four times. And I had such grief from my husband—I had to lie to him, and to my daughter, and... and, finally, to Andrei Petrovich himself—who suffered a lot. It's horrible to have to act like that. Like they say in that song, 'What were we struggling for?'"

"To hell, to hell, to hell with him," Margarita Nikolaevna would answer calmly. "I understand everything. He abandoned you and you're in despair. When a woman is in despair she must first of all say 'to hell with him.'"

"But I bought a hat with a dove on it especially for him."

"As far as that's concerned, just amortize the hat and the dove along with it. You did like him once, you know."

"Yes, but you know it's not the same."

"Thank God, it's not the same."

"And do you know the bastard is making advances to Krotova now? She's a fool and she's ugly and I don't like her at all."

"Does a man have to choose a rival who fits your taste?"

"Well, it's not so insulting if he's unfaithful with a beauty. But here he's traded me in for a cow."

"On the contrary, it's worse if they leave you for a beauty. With a cow there's still a chance he'll remember you with pleasure, but with a beauty, if he remembers you at all, it will only be to your disadvantage."

"Anyway, this is all very hard to endure," the abandoned one sighed.

"Come on now, was he so very interesting, this guy?"

"Him? Interesting? You're making fun of me. He is insignificant, and such a bastard! Slanting shoulders, crooked legs, no ethics whatsoever, the mentality of a bovine. It was hellish, utter boredom with him. I myself don't know how I ever stood him for so long. Four times—just think!—four times I dined with him. I had a real fog over my eyes. And the dinners were long—five courses, plus coffee. You know, I had to endure all that. He never said a word, just ate. He chewed like a sheep—his lower jaw moved from side to side. And on top of all that, he had no ethics whatsoever. I can't understand why I'm suffering like this from his betrayal. It would be different if he were handsome, romantic and genteel. But he's such trash, and anyway, he cooled towards me. Tepid trash, that's all he is! And here I am upset. Whatever for?"

"My dear," said Margarita Nikolaevna. "If you're sitting under a tree and a little bird ruins your hat, you could care less what kind of bird it is—a nightingale or a crow. So whether a Shakespearian Romeo or a salesman from a shoe store betrayed you, the damage is the same."

"Well, I still think it's harder to bear an insult from a salesman."

"On the contrary. At least you can say that the boor can't understand a sensitive nature or appreciate true grace and beauty."

"So what should I do?"

"Say to hell with him, my dear. Otherwise—you already understand—there's only trouble and expense. An abandoned woman will first of all run off to an *institut de beauté*. First, to elevate her spirits, and second, in the hopes that if the bastard sees her with a new, fresh look, he'll sigh and change his mind.

A Woman's Lot

"After that the abandoned woman, with that same goal in mind, will run to the dressmaker and the milliner and waste money on her wardrobe. So, choose for yourself. Grief will pass of its own accord in the end. You're not really thinking of bemoaning the treachery of such an insignificant type for the rest of your life, are you?"

"Of course not! I'd be a fool if I did!"

"Well, that's what I'm saying. It will all pass, but in the meantime you'll be paying good money for dresses. And hats. And all for no reason at all. So it's better to say to hell with him from the start."

"All that's fine and dandy," the abandoned woman sighed, "but the nerves are upset by this kind of loss."

"Just give him some of his own medicine. He was unfaithful, so now you be unfaithful, too."

"But you can't just pick up a new one so quickly. And anyway, the echoes of the past are still reverberating."

"No matter. It's easy to deal with echoes. Take a little valerian and they fade away."

"I took some already."

"Take a little more."

"I took a little more."

"Then go to a nerve doctor."

The abandoned woman fell to thinking. "Liza Rakanova went to one," she said.

"Well, did it help?"

"Very much so."

"What was the matter with her?"

"Her husband made off with a ballerina. She suffered terribly, of course. It was mainly insulting that the ballerina leapt so heavily. Even the critics pointed that out. Liza suffered especially from that circumstance. So she went to a nerve doctor. She told him about her trouble. He felt terribly sorry for her, even patted her hand, and spoke enthusiastically about valerian. After a while he sees that his advice isn't being taken and he says, just like you did right now: 'If he's such a bastard as to be unfaithful to you, you just be unfaithful to him.'

"She, of course, cries, 'Oh, oh! How can I, I still love him so much, I can't even imagine doing something like that.'

"So this doctor, he says: 'There's nothing so terrible about it.' And bang-bang, he up and kisses her. 'It's not really so terrible now, is it?' "

"What is this 'bang-bang'?" asked Margarita Nikolaevna, surprised at the strange sound effects.

"I just said it like that to express the suddenness of the act."

"Well, and then what?"

"Well, nothing. She divorced her husband and got married."

"To the doctor?"

"No. Where did you get such an idea? To some engineer."

"Yes, nerve doctors, they sometimes help a lot," Margarita Nikolaevna said thoughtfully. "Science is making great strides."

"Only I don't know if she's happy in her second marriage. If she meets up with another ladies' man, her happiness may not last long."

Margarita Nikolaevna looked at the abandoned woman very sternly and said: "Now, my dear, you leave that topic alone. I won't allow you to insult ladies' men."

The abandoned one was indignant. "Well, what good is there in them? Today he's chasing me, yesterday he was chasing another, and tomorrow he'll be chasing a third. It's disgraceful, you know. And the day after tomorrow he'll be after yet another."

"And that's how it should be," Margarita Nikolaevna calmly said. "If there were no such thing as a ladies' man, you'd never have been chased in the first place. And really, for us average women, the only joy is to be had from ladies' men. How can you possibly extol a man who loves only one woman? He's the most dreadful type! It's all very convenient for him, of course. He bestirs himself once, falls in love, and then there's no more bother, while you sit and suffer. What a sight he is! And how boring! He doesn't look at anyone, he mutters to himself under his breath, he goes to bed at ten o'clock.

"A ladies' man will finish off his cognac and just be warming up for his evening's machinations. A compliment to the right, a compliment to the left, a wicked eye on the one across the table. 'I may be silent,' his eyes say, 'but I'm suffering.' And everyone is happy and feels the heat.

"But a one-woman man is inaccessible. Don't expect any compliments from him—he considers a compliment a betrayal of the ideal. If you joke with him, he'll look at you distrustfully from under his brows. He'll blush and begin to rummage for his hat.

"A one-woman man will go home earlier than everyone else. And at home his suffering wife, having sent him off alone on the excuse that she had a headache, will have to dash around picking up someone else's cigarette butts and putting everything in the room back in order. So you see, from a one-woman man you get only anxiety and grief.

"A ladies' man doesn't sit at home. He's always running off somewhere. Therefore his wife values his presence, while she puts his absence to good use for herself.

"Besides, a ladies' man is an absolutely harmless creature. He'll never cause a tragedy. Everything is easy for him. He willingly forgives infidelities, doesn't always even notice them. He doesn't immerse himself in suffering. He is jealous exactly as much as is necessary to gratify a woman. Not that he pretends or holds himself back—he's just like that by his nature.

"A one-woman man loves to philosophize and make conclusions, and if something happens, he immediately finds fault and goes and shoots his wife and children. He's always trying to kill himself, too, but for some reason he never succeeds, although he won't slip up with the wife and children. Afterwards he'll explain by saying that he was used to worrying first and foremost about his beloved family, and only then about himself. 'I live somehow—just how, I don't know. I myself always played second fiddle.'

"Yes, dear," Margarita Nikolaevna ended her speech. "Never curse the ladies' men, but fear those who love only one."

The abandoned one thought, sighed, and doubtfully asked: "Maybe I should fall in love with Shura's husband? He likes me."

"With that fool Mitenka? Never! It's a violation of the tenth commandment."

"The tenth? You mean the seventh. 'Don't commit adultery' is the seventh commandment."

"It may be there in the seventh in a general sense, but the tenth commands directly: 'Thou shalt not covet thy neighbor's ass.' Enticing Mitenka is just the same as taking someone else's ass, you know. That's just not nice."

"Then how . . ." the abandoned one began again.

But Margarita Nikolaevna stopped her with a powerful gesture and said full of feeling: "Say to hell with him!"

An Atmosphere of Love

The beginning of this story is rather banal: a certain lady decided to invite to her home only those people who, in her opinion, loved her and would therefore not cause her any unpleasant moments.

But it's not so easy to gather such a group of people as you may think. Perhaps you know that a certain Ivan Andreevich feels strongly obliged to you, but whether he's grateful to you is another question. Perhaps he can't stand you precisely because he's obliged to you. Doesn't that sometimes occur?

And so the lady thought for a long time and decided she could invite only those people who had at one time shared with her pieces of their souls. A person never forgets the spot where he once buried a small piece of his soul. He often returns to it, circles around it, tries to paw at it a little from above, like a dog with a bone.

This is even truer of men. Women are ungrateful creatures. They rarely remember with warmth a person who is no longer with them. They can recall someone they had three children with and lived with for five years like this: "And that idiot actually imagined I was capable of being intimate with him!"

Men relate more gratefully to the bright memory of a past romance.

Anyway, the lady we're talking about decided to invite four cavaliers. Two of them belonged to her past, one to her present, and one to her future.

The first of those belonging to the past was none other than her former husband. At one time he had suffered greatly. Then he had remarried and switched from a state of suffering to one of serene friendship for his ex-wife, and when he became bored with his new wife, he again felt a surge of tenderness for his former. This love was expressed by the fact that he gave her a one-tenth share in the National Lottery and sometimes came to lunch with her. His name was Andrei Andreich.

The second man from her past was the one on whose account they'd divorced. His affections had long ago evolved to simple friendship for her, but he was still full of adoration and gratefulness for the unforgettable pages... from his point of view, of course. She invited him over in rainy weather for quiet conversations and reading aloud. He spoke beautifully. He played the guitar, sighed, and borrowed small amounts of money. His name was Sergei Nikolaich.

The one belonging to the present was Aleksei Petrovich. Like the hero of a popular novel, he was always anxious, suspicious and jealous, always ready to cause a scandal. There could be no doubt as to his feelings for her.

The man of the future was the dancer, Vovochka. Vovochka was still in the phase of dreams and desires, in the epoch of compliments and glances. He was exceptionally nice.

In sum, the whole company, the whole major chord of four notes, promised to be pleasant, joyful, elevating to her mood and attentive to her feminine powers. In every woman of certain years (it would be more precise to call them "uncertain") there are moments when it is necessary to lift the spirit and have a good time. And nothing lifts this fallen spirit better than an atmosphere of love. To feel herself admired, to feel infatuated eyes following her every move—then everything in the sensitive female soul (the two kilos recently gained and the wrinkles noticed at the corners of the mouth) melts away, the shoulders straighten, the eyes begin to sparkle, and the woman can look boldly to her future, which is sitting right there. She jauntily crosses her legs and lights a cigarette.

And so, the lady we're talking about—this lady's name was Marya Artemevna—invited these four men to dinner.

The first to arrive, personifying the present, was Aleksei Petrovich. When he learned who else was invited, his face tightened in obvious disapproval.

"What a strange idea!" he said. "Can these people really be of any special significance? But that is your business, I suppose."

Aleksei became pensive and gloomy, and only the name Vovochka brought a smile to his face. "A nice young man. And quite serious, despite his profession."

Though Marya Artemevna was a bit surprised, she concealed it. The evening began quite well, and everything promised to go as smoothly as a train on a new-laid track.

Her former husband brought candy. It was such a sweet gesture that she whispered to him involuntarily: "*Merci*, kitten."

The second representative of the past, Sergei Nikolaich, brought her violets, and that was so tender of him that she involuntarily whispered to him, too: "*Merci*, kitten."

Vovochka didn't bring anything and was so boyishly embarrassed on seeing the gifts, that out of tenderness she whispered to him, too: "*Merci*, kitten."

In short, everything was charming.

Of course, Andrei Andreich looked askance at Sergei Nikolaich's violets—but that was completely natural. And Andrei Andreich's candy grated on Sergei Nikolaich's nerves—but that was completely understandable. It goes without saying that both the flowers and the candy were unpleasant to Aleksei Petrovich—but that too was completely legitimate. Vovochka sulked—but that was so amusing!

Trifles—let them be jealous!

Marya Artemevna felt like a merry bee, the queen of a hive amid the buzzing love of drones.

They sat down to eat: cabbage soup with cheese tarts, cognac and vodka. Everyone grew warm and began to chatter.

Rosy and animated, Marya Artemevna thought: "What an inspiration it was to invite only these tried and true friends! They all love me and feel jealous, and their common feelings unite them among themselves."

"The cheese tarts aren't quite done," Aleksei Petrovich, the representative of the present, suddenly noted, raising his brows significantly.

"I'll say!" her former husband joined in goodnaturedly. "Don't be insulted, Manurochka, but you're not much of a hostess."

"Well, well, no matter," Marya Artemevna cheerfully stopped them. "They're not all that bad. I'm eating them with great pleasure."

"*That* doesn't necessarily mean anything..." Sergei Nikolaich, the one on whose account they'd been divorced, said rather irritably. "You've never been noted either for your taste or your discrimination."

"Women in general . . ." Vovochka suddenly entered the conversation, then stopped short, blushed, and fell silent.

Marya Artemevna burst into laughter. "Gentlemen, really, how cross you all are!"

She wanted to cut short this tedious conversation and once again create a tender, comfortable atmosphere of love.

But it wasn't so easy to do.

"*We're* cross?" asked her former husband. "That's the usual female way of transferring guilt onto others. She's responsible for the raw dough, but we're the ones who are guilty. We, it turns out, are cross."

But Marya Artemevna did not want to give up.

"Vovochka," she said, smiling coquettishly at the representative of her future. "Vovochka, do you agree? Do you also believe it's impossible to eat my cheese tarts?"

Vovochka, under the influence of her tender smile, was about to start smiling himself, when suddenly the voice of Aleksei Petrovich was heard:

"Monsieur Vovochka is too well brought up to answer you truthfully. On the other hand, he's too cultured to eat this dreadful concoction. I hope you're not insulted, my dear?"

Vovochka frowned to show the complexity of his situation. Marya Artemevna smiled ingratiatingly at each one in turn, and the dinner continued.

"Well now," she said cheerfully and brightly. "I hope that this *matelote* of eel will make you forget about the tarts."

Once again she smiled coquettishly, but no one was paying attention to her any more. Her former husband began to talk with Aleksei Petrovich about bank business. Their conversation began to interest Sergei Nikolaich so much that the hostess had to ask him twice if he wanted salad. The first time he didn't answer at all, and the second time he growled: "All right, I'll have some! Now leave me alone!"

Vovochka heard this unexpected retort. He pouted and blushed.

Marya Artemevna felt that her future was in danger.

"Vovochka," she said very softly, "do you like my jabot? I put it on especially for you."

Vovochka cast a sidelong look at the jabot and growled: "It makes your neck look fat."

Then he turned away.

There was nothing to be done with him.

Meanwhile, the other three were becoming fast friends. The hostess had ceased to exist for them. They paid no attention to her questions or her food. Only once did her former husband speak to her, and that was to ask if she had any mineral water. He called her Sonechka for some reason, not even realizing his error.

These three had shifted the conversation long ago from bank business to politics, and their views coincided to a surprising extent. Only once did a small difference appear. Andrei Andreich had heard from a certain Frenchman that the Bolsheviks would fall in September, whereas Sergei Nikolaich knew for himself that they were supposed to have fallen last March, but out of carelessness and lack of organization they were, of course, late.

From politics they moved on to jokes, which they whispered in each other's ears, laughing long and loud.

When they got tired of whispering, Andrei Andreich said to Marya Artemevna: "You, sweetheart, would be better off looking after the coffee in the kitchen, otherwise it will turn out like your cheese tarts did. We'll just sit here and chat while you're gone. I'm surprised that you never think of anything for yourself."

Everyone laughed approvingly at these words.

Marya Artemevna was very insulted. She went into her bedroom and had herself a little cry.

When she returned to the dining room, she found that her guests had already risen and, declining coffee, were hurrying off.

"We're going to Montparnasse, to a cafe somewhere, for a little air," Aleksei Petrovich coldly explained to his hostess, looking somewhere beyond her.

Talking cheerfully, they began to descend the stairs.

"Vovochka!" Marya Artemevna stopped her dancer, almost in despair. "Vovochka, it's still early. Please stay!"

But Vovochka grinned crookedly and mumbled: "Forgive me, Marya Artemevna, it would be awkward in front of your men."

And with a leap he bounded down the stairs.

An Easter Story

Most people probably remember the traditional holiday stories that used to be printed at Christmas and Easter. And those who haven't read them know them second hand, since they've been parodied so many times.

The stories had certain fixed themes.

For the Christmas story there was always a freezing little boy or a poor man's child at a rich man's Christmas party.

For the Easter story it was customary to relate the return of the prodigal husband to his wife, left languishing alone over the *kulich*.* Or the return of the prodigal wife to her abandoned husband soaking the *baba au rhum* with his lonely tears. Reconciliation and forgiveness are achieved to the ringing of the Easter bells.

Such were the carefully chosen, established themes.

Why the stories all had to be like that, no one knows. The husband and wife could just as easily have been reconciled on Christmas Eve, and the poor boy could just as touchingly have broken his fast among rich children at Easter as at Christmas.

But these themes have taken such root that it's impossible even to consider changing them. Indignant readers would write indignant letters, and the magazine's circulation would plummet.

Even great writers have resigned themselves to these themes. One such writer was commissioned to write a Christmas story—so he wrote one. When they commissioned an Easter story from him, he knew what was expected of him then, too.

Even as a refined a writer as Fyodor Sologub** wrote on Easter themes, with spouses reuniting to the ringing of bells. However, there was hidden irony in Sologub, and he sometimes liked to give the standard theme a twist, as if mocking himself and the publishers who were paying him at the time.

But now I'll tell you a genuine Easter story, the author of which is Life itself. Just imagine Life, having read its fill of sentimental Easter fabrications, declaring: "No, dear writers, I never work out in such pat resolutions. It's just not my style! But if you want, I'll portray myself for you as I really am."

This humble scribe will try to transmit the story just as it was told by Life.

Kulich is a sweet Russian Easter bread baked in a cylindrical mold. (Trans.)

**Fyodor Sologub (1863-1927) is best known for his novel *The Petty Demon*. A Symbolist, he dealt with the problem of Good and Evil. (Trans.)

All About Love

****

Nina Nikolaevna pressed closer to Andreev. He took her by the hand and began to elbow his way through the crowd.

"There are always so many people at these matins!" complained Nina Nikolaevna. "You can't see anything, you can't hear anything, you can't even get into the church. You just stamp your feet from the cold outside, and you can never spot people you know."

"There are a lot of foreigners here," said Andreev. "They're curious about the service."

A low-pitched bell rang out.

The faces of the crowd, illuminated by the warm pink flames of candles, looked very strange, with dark gaping holes for eyes, wide arching brows, and holes for mouths.

Huge "suns" from the movie equipment lit up the crowds on the cathedral steps and the slowly flowing Procession of the Cross.

"Let's go home," said Nina Nikolaevna. "It's starting to drizzle."

"Do you want to break the fast together today?" asked Andreev.

"I don't have anything special to eat—just some *kulich, paskha*,* ham and sausage from the Russian shop."

"What else do you need! That's already a lavish feast! Does this mean you're inviting me?"

Nina Nikolaevna and Andreev got along very well together by nature. Maybe because they saw each other only in the evenings, after work, when there was hardly enough time to express tender feelings, let alone ugly ones.

Nina Nikolaevna was very nice and easy to be with. Andreev was an uncomplicated man, not at all ravaged by uncertainties or spiritual needs. He lived simply. He ate, drank, worked and took his girl to the movies. He wore fresh collars and even cleaned his nails.

A man with such wonderful qualities—and one who appeared in Nina Nikolaevna's life at such an opportune time, at just the moment when such a man was needed—could not help but capture her heart. Their fatal meeting occurred just as Nina Nikolaevna's husband, a neurotic of the most annoying type (a crank, a nagger and a whiner), announced to her that they would never understand one another. Then he left, slamming the door.

Why he made such an ineffectual statement so near the end of the performance we don't know. In fact, they had been quarrelling

---

**Paskha is the traditional Easter dessert of molded pot cheese which is served with *kulich*. (Trans.)

about the fact that they understood each other too well: Nina understood that he was a loafer and an idler who was angry not to have the money to sit in a bistro for hours on end, where he could unravel all kinds of nonsensical, peevish thoughts in front of some chance listener; he understood that she wanted to dress up and go to the movies. And in neither of them was there anything more to understand.

So when the door slammed behind him, she remembered only that she had failed to reproach him for the time he was sick last fall and she hadn't been able to sleep for three nights. She jumped up and flung open the door to shout down the stairwell that he was an ungrateful pig, and in doing so she bumped right into a charming gentleman in multicolored pajamas, who was placing his boots on his doorstep.

As he explained later, he was struck by Nina Nikolaevna's excited face.

"An indescribable expression and temperament!" he thought.

The very next morning he timidly knocked at her door and asked if it would bother her if he smoked at night.

She expressed amazement. "Can it really make any difference through the wall?"

"Oh, don't say that!" he exclaimed. "Parisian buildings are not at all sturdy. The concrete here is so porous that it absorbs everything. And I would never forgive myself if you were to suffer on my account."

And so it went. By the next day he knew that she no longer believed in love and would remain alone forever, and she knew that he had never loved and never would.

Having made their feelings clear, with her consent he moved into the apartment on the other side of her room, because this was an adjoining apartment.

Nina Nikolaevna's husband never did return.

He wrote her two long letters, in which he informed her that he could never forgive her—for what exactly, he didn't explain. Instead, he expounded in great detail his views on the psychology of modern man. He demanded absolute perfection, and that as soon as possible. "The world is suffocating!" he exclaimed.

Nina Nikolaevna did not care for his letters at all.

"What a dummy," she thought. "I'd rather he wrote whether or not he's found a job."

Time passed. Andreev, with whom there was no time to argue, began to seem a bit bland.

"It's movies and more movies. He has no spiritual needs at all," she thought, already with some irritation.

All About Love

Her husband's letters began to appeal to her more and more.

"He really was an exceptional man. Maybe I *was* the one to blame?"

She didn't have any pictures of her husband. There was only the old card from their courting days portraying him with inspired eyes and a tuft of hair across his forehead. Looking at the card, Nina Nikolaevna gradually began to forget the plump, sallow face of more recent years.

****

The hotel doors were not yet locked when Nina Nikolaevna and Andreev came home. Catching sight of Nina Nikolaevna, the desk clerk said in an undertone, giving Andreev a sidelong glance: "Monsieur is sitting in your room, Madame."

At first Nina Nikolaevna did not understand to whom the clerk was referring.

"Monsieur—your husband," the girl explained impatiently, again looking askance at Andreev.

Nina Nikolaevna froze. "Go to your own room," she said under her breath. "We'll straighten things out later. My husband has returned."

Andreev started to rush over to her. He started to say something, but instead he only spread his hands in confusion and ran up the stairs, taking them two at a time.

Nina Nikolaevna, with a heavily beating heart, began slowly to climb the stairs. Closing her eyes, she stood for a moment before her door.

"Returned! Returned! He's returned! My God! I think I love him!"

She opened the door and stopped short....

At the table a plump, sallow man was sitting and eating ham with gusto.

"Forgive me," he said calmly. "I couldn't wait any longer, so I began to nibble."

She looked at him in confusion and didn't know what to do. So she took off her hat. She placed it on the bed. Then she moved a chair up to the table. She sat down.

He ran his eyes up and down her, opened his mouth, began to smoke, and asked in a business-like way: "Do you have any tea? I'd like a cup."

"Right away," she said in a trembling voice and disappeared behind the partition.

An Easter Story

"How amazing!" she thought. "It's just like a fairy tale! He has returned on Easter night. And how proud he's acting! But what will happen with Andreev now? A tragedy, no doubt... He returned! It's like a dream... He ate my ham... It's like a dream. What is this feeling—love, or what?"

When she came back to the table he was chewing pensively on some *kulich* spread with *paskha*.

"So how are you?" he asked rather indifferently. Not waiting for an answer, he continued: "I've done a lot of thinking and have decided to forgive you. In the final analysis, you're not to blame if your parents were stupid and passed that unfortunate characteristic on to you. What can you do? If you were very pretty and could conceal your spiritual defects with beauty, things would be easier, of course. Oh, you needn't be insulted. I'm not saying this to insult you, but for you to understand your position in the world. No doubt you never thought about your position in the world. A creature like you, in order to justify its existence, must be sacrificial. You should serve a creature of a higher order, a chosen personality."

He plopped himself into the armchair, inhaled his cigarette, and sticking his hands into his pockets, continued.

"Right now I'm working out a certain plan on a grandiose European scale. It needs strong and quick development. Try to follow my train of thought, if you can. Now where was I?... Oh, yes, strong and quick development. On a grandiose European scale. I'm not thinking of living with you, of course. Philistinism would engulf me again. But I've forgiven you and now I'm giving you the opportunity to be useful to me and to my work... In short, do you have fifty francs?"

Nina Nikolaevna opened the window to let the tobacco smoke drift out. She listened. She seemed to hear the ringing Easter bells still resounding in the air. No, it was just an automobile horn.

She cleared the table.

Her cheeks were burning, but her soul was calm and at peace. A schoolboy who has long been threatened with punishment probably feels the same way when finally thrashed.

She swept the crumbs off the tablecloth, removed the dirty plate, touched up the surface of the *paskha* to make it look whole again, disguising the fact that a healthy piece had already been eaten. Then she straightened her hair and knocked at Andreev's door.

He answered immediately and appeared in her apartment, sulky and offended, not knowing how to behave.

She seated him at the table and, having placed a fatal expression on her face (brows raised, eyes lowered, lips compressed), she talked until morning about her husband, about how the madman had sobbed, begging her to forgive him and allow him to return, and trying to tempt her with his excellent job and large salary: "Fifty francs a day guaranteed."

But she had turned him down. And if he shoots himself, then "Believe me, not a single fiber of my face will twitch."

Andreev looked at her face, from which powder was peeling, and thought: "This is a fatal woman. I'd better keep my distance."

The Shopgirl's Tale

What injustices there are in our woman's fate! You'd never find them in the animal kingdom. Take that incident with Berta Karlovna. Did you ever hear of anything like it? You couldn't imagine it if you tried.

I know all about it because it happened before my very eyes. Berta Karlovna and I arrived in Paris together. She, Auntie, and I. As soon as we arrived we began to look for a place to hang our hats.

Auntie found work before the rest of us—in a laundry, picking up stitches on stockings. She advised me to take up the same work, because if the laundry's a large one, you can earn twenty francs a day. Half of it you have to give back to the proprietor, of course, but ten francs—that's guaranteed.

But I wasn't tempted by that kind of work. Some treat for a young girl of thirty to be stewed in other people's stockings! All around lies the capital of the world, while you work like a draft horse from dawn till dark in some laundry.

We talked to our own people, Russians, who had arrived before us and were already established. They started right in with their opinions.

"That's no kind of career for a modern single girl," they would say. "Nowadays there is only one career in the world."

"Which is that?" we asked.

"Hollywood."

"Huh? What's that?"

But they only repeated, "Hollywood."

We thought it might be some man or other. But the Parisians explained everything to us.

"First of all, off with your eyebrows! You've got to pluck your brows bare, then paint them in again. You have to bleach your hair and make up your face. And then, if you're lucky, you can get fixed up in Hollywood."

It soon became clear that in Paris there existed a feminine fate even without Hollywood: rich Englishmen, once they attain a respectable age, begin to love the Russian soul. And if a face made up and plucked to fit the Russian soul is added into the bargain, the girl's fate is not just settled—it's settled lawfully.

I listened and listened to these exhortations, and I said to my Berta Karlovna: "You, my dear, can do as you like, but I'm going to aim for Hollywood. A girl can earn a million a day there."

But Berta stood firm.

Incidentally, Berta is quite homely. She's large and her spine is curved like a cat's. Her shoulder blades stick out, her big hands are like rakes, and her face is long, with a moustache. Despite her name, she doesn't look German—her brows are too thick. And even if you bleached her and plucked her, she'd only turn out worse.

So for her there was no road to Hollywood. The road to an Englishman was hardly open to her, either, because she doesn't have a Russian soul. Even though she was born in Russia, she doesn't speak the language quite right. She's always adding something like "in any case." As if it weren't really Russian she's speaking.

Well, I pawned my warm overcoat and Mamochka's little ring, and I went to the hairdresser's to be fixed up Hollywood style. It seemed ugly, since I wasn't used to it: white hair, face blue-grey from the hair, in place of brows—puffiness. But the look was stylish and that, as they say, is the main thing.

My friend Bertochka and I began to look for jobs. At first I decided not to rush things—in case they invited me to Hollywood. It wasn't worth starting work only to quit right away. That would just strain my nerves.

So I sat around for about two weeks and saw that things weren't going too well. No one even cared that my eyebrows were plucked. And I'd forked over forty-six francs plus two for tea to the hairdresser for all that Hollywood. I had to skimp on food and drink.

Berta Karlovna found herself a job. As a cashier in a candy store. She was very satisfied with it. Her only complaint concerned a draft from the door—in three weeks she'd already gotten two swollen cheeks from it.

I felt very insulted that I—such a darling, such a fashion queen!—was sitting without a job, while the moustached Berta had done so well for herself.

One day she suggested, "If you want me to, I'll try to fix you up as a salesgirl."

That stung me. "I didn't prepare myself for that kind of career! I'm young and pretty. Why should I spend my whole life wrapping candies for other people's mouths?"

But Berta answered, "No one knows her fate. I recently met a salesgirl at the spa. She was from a candy store, too. One day an Indian king dropped into her store. The minute he saw her, he bought a million and a half's worth of candy and plop! right onto his knees: 'Be my wife,' he cries, 'otherwise I won't live and you won't live, it will be the end!' The owners were frightened. They sent for an interpreter, who set everything straight, and the next day they celebrated a wedding.

The Shopgirl's Tale

"In any case," Berta concluded, "millions of kings of all kinds visit candy stores. Maybe one will become interested in you."

Well, I thought, why not start with the candy trade? You have to start somewhere.

And I just happened to be lucky. The store needed another salesgirl, Berta Karlovna recommended me, and I was hired.

There were two others besides me and Berta. And they both resembled me: made-up, plucked, with white hair and cheeks blue-grey from the hair. Really, we were just like sisters. All very sweet and utterly Hollywood. Behind the cash register stood our huge, bony, thick-browed Berta, thundering away, and her cheeks were still swollen. What a sight! Really, she's not a woman, but some sexless creature. Not even suited for the candy trade. With candy you need a little smile, frivolity, a pleasant smell, violet cologne. Well, God be with her, every person has to live.

One day a greyhaired gentleman came in. He was very attractive. He wore new gloves. One of our mademoiselles whispered to me: 'He came in his own car!' I just loaded him with candy. And of course I smiled, and I picked out the candy with my fingers crooked so gracefully that, really, it should have been set to music. He bought a pound of chocolate fondant and a half pound of croquant. (A very reserved type!) Then he went over to the register and looked attentively at our Berta. He added up the bill himself and looked at her in such a way that he missed his wallet when he put his money away.

When he left, we—the mademoiselles—began to talk among ourselves, agreeing that it's not good to have a cashier like Berta. She's a real scarecrow with one cheek all tied up in bandages. But it really was none of our business, especially none of mine. She's my friend, and she got me the job.

About two weeks later our reserved gentleman appeared once again. He bought a pound of *truffes au chocolat*, again paying no attention to us mademoiselles. But as he approached the register, he fixed his gaze again on Berta. Suddenly he said: "Is your cheek still swollen? There must be a draft on you."

Berta shrugged her shoulders. "Yes," she answered, "there's a draft, but what can I do about it?"

He shook his head and left.

Well, we thought, they'll fire our Berta. The customers are already noticing that she has an unseemly swollen cheek.

A few days later this same gentleman dropped in again. He bought a pound of fondant. At the register he asked Berta: "Is that a new inflammation or still the same one?"

I don't know what she answered, only suddenly he leaned over, took her by the hand, and said: "You should find a job where there won't be a draft on you." And he added: "Think my words over well."

With that, he left the store, got into his automobile, and rolled off.

We were all terribly surprised. What could it mean? "You should find another job." Maybe he meant that she should clear out of there?

We didn't understand at all. Berta cried all evening.

But what do you think? The next day our gentleman appeared again. This time he didn't buy a thing. He went right over to the register and whispered something to Berta. Berta turned red as a lobster and began to wave her hands around. Then she cried, "Yes!" and started to laugh and cry like a cow.

The gentleman calmly took a jewelry case out of his pocket, opened it, and removed a ring with a stone in it. He caught her hand, put the ring on her, and very elegantly announced to us: "Allow me to introduce Mad'moiselle . . . What's your name?"

She cried, "Berta!"

"Mademoiselle Berta, my bride. I'm Merlan, a doorknob manufacturer. I have a warm apartment where her splendid cheek won't bother her any more."

Well, what do you say to that?

Of course, he's not a king, but by today's standards, at least his position is stable.

Now just let them tell me about plucked brows and the rest of that Hollywood stuff! Just let them try! I know what I'll say to them!

A Wise Man

He's skinny and tall, his head is narrow and bald, and there's a wise expression on his face.

He talks only about practical topics, with no little jokes or anecdotes, no little smiles. If he does grin, then his grin is always ironic, the corners of his mouth curling down.

He occupies a modest position in the emigration, selling perfume and herring door to door. The perfumes smell like herring, and the herring, like perfume.

He's a bad businessman. He convinces unconvincingly: "You say the perfume stinks? Well, after all, it's cheap. You'd fork out sixty francs for the same perfume in a store, but it only costs nine from me. Maybe it smells bad now, but you'll get used to it. Man can get used to anything."

"What? The herring smells like cologne? Don't worry, it won't harm the taste. It's not important. Look, they say the Germans eat a cheese that smells like a dead body. No problem. They're not bothered by it. Doesn't it make them sick? I don't know, no one ever complained about it. And no one ever died of nausea . . . at least no one complained that he died."

His complexion is grey, his brows red. They're red and they quiver. He loves to talk about his life, perceiving it as a model of sensible and proper behavior. Talking about it, he preaches, but at the same time he displays mistrust at quick-wittedness and receptiveness.

"Our last name is Vuryugin. Not Voryugin, as many people take the liberty of joking,* but Vuryugin, from an unknown root. We lived in Taganrog. And what style we lived in! No Frenchman could have such a life, not even in his wildest dreams. Six horses, two cows. A kitchen garden, a landed estate. Father kept a shop. What kind of shop? Well, he had everything. You want a brick—you get a brick. You want Lenten butter—here's butter, if you please. You want a sheepskin coat—you get a coat. He even had ready-made clothes. And what clothes! Not like they have here—you wear them a year and they turn shiny. We had materials you couldn't even dream of here. Sturdy fabrics, with a pile. And the cut was smart, wide. Any artist would wear our clothes—he wouldn't be making a mistake. Our clothes were fashionable. Here the fashion's a bit weak, I must say. Last summer the shops here displayed brown leather boots. In

---

*The root of the name Voryugin is *vor* or "thief." (Trans.)

all the stores. Ach! The latest fashion! Well, I look and I just shake my head. I wore boots like that twenty years ago in Taganrog. That's when it was—twenty years ago—and only now has the style reached them here. Who says the French are so fashionable? Hah!

"And the women here, how they dress! Did our women ever wear such pancakes on their heads? They'd have been downright embarrassed to go out in public with pancakes like that on. Our women dressed fashionably, chicly. But here they don't have an inkling of style.

"It's boring here. Terribly boring. Nothing but metro and movies. Did we ever rush around like that in Taganrog? Several hundred thousand people pass through the Paris metro every day. And you're going to assure me that all of them are travelling on business? Well, go ahead and lie, but remember there are limits to my gullibility. Three hundred thousand people a day and all on business? Just where are all these businesses of theirs? What business do they engage in? In trade? In trade, I beg your pardon, there's a depression going on. In jobs, too, I beg your pardon, there's a depression. So where, may I ask, is the business to which three hundred thousand people rush day and night on the metro, goggling their eyes? I'm amazed, I take a respectful attitude towards this statistic, but I don't believe it.

"Of course, living in a foreign country is difficult, and there's a lot you don't understand. Especially if you're alone. During the day you work, but in the evenings you just go crazy. Sometimes in the evening you go over to the washstand, you look at yourself in the mirror and you say: 'Vuryugin, Vuryugin! Is it you who is a hero and a knight in shining armor? Is it you who is Vuryugin and Son, Inc., who symbolizes those six horses and those two cows? Your life is solitary and you're all dried up, like a flower without a root.'

"And now I must tell you that one day I decided to fall in love. As they say, the decision was signed, sealed and delivered. On the landing of our hotel, "Trésor," lived a young lady—very nice and, between you and me, quite pretty. A widow. She had a five-year-old son, a great kid. That little boy was really great.

"The lady wasn't bad off. She earned a little by sewing, so she didn't complain much. The others, you know—our refugees—you invite one to tea, and the whole time, like some stingy bookkeeper, she keeps on counting and recounting to you: 'Ach, they didn't pay me fifty there, and here they didn't pay up sixty, and the room costs two hundred a month, and the metro three francs a day.' They add and subtract—it makes you sick. When you're with a lady it's important that she says something nice about *you*, not about her accounts. Well, this lady was something special. She was always

A Wise Man

humming, but at the same time she wasn't frivolous. On the contrary, she had spiritual needs, an approach to life. Once she noticed on my overcoat a button hanging by a thread, and without saying a word, she brought a needle and sewed it on.

"Well, you know, the further it went, the more involved I became. I decided to fall in love. And her little boy was great. I like to deal with everything seriously. Especially something like this. You have to be logical. I didn't have trifles in mind, but lawful marriage. And by the way, I asked her whether she had her own teeth. Even though she was young, all kinds of things might have happened, you know. There was a certain teacher in Taganrog. She was also young, but it turned out she had a glass eye.

"So I took a good look at my lady and I weighed everything completely.

"I decided I could marry her. But then a certain unexpected circumstance opened my eyes. It showed me that I—as a decent and conscientious, even a noble man—could never marry her. You know, it seems so insignificant now, but it set my whole life back a notch.

"Here's how it was: One evening we were sitting very cozily at her place, reminiscing about what kinds of soups there were in Russia. We had counted fourteen, but we'd forgotten pea soup. The situation became quite funny. That is, she laughed; I don't like to laugh. I would sooner be plagued with a defective memory. Anyway, we were sitting and reminiscing about our past power. The little boy was there, too.

" 'Give me a caramel, *maman*,' he said.

"She answered: 'No more, you've already eaten three.'

"But he kept pestering her—gimme, gimme, gimme.

"So I said in a serious tone, even though I was joking: 'Come over here, I'm going to spank you.'

"Then my lady went and said the fatal words: 'Are you kidding? You're such a softie, you couldn't spank him!'

"The floor dropped out from under my feet. To take upon myself the upbringing of an infant, at just the age when they have to be whipped from time to time, was absolutely impossible in light of my character. I couldn't take that upon myself. Could I ever really whip him? No, I couldn't. I can't fight. And what then? Ruin a child, the son of your favorite woman?

" 'Forgive me, Anna Pavlovna,' I said. 'Forgive me, but our marriage is a utopia in which we'll all perish. Because I cannot be a real father and disciplinarian to your son. What you say is only too true. Frankly, I couldn't ever whip him, not even once.'

"I spoke with great reserve—not a single fiber of my face twitched. Well, maybe my voice was slightly muffled, but I can swear to the fibers.

"She, of course—oh! Love and all that, you won't have to whip the child, he's so good, she kept saying.

" 'He's good now,' I said, 'he's good . . . but he'll be bad. I beg you not to insist. Be strong. Remember that I can't spank. It's not right to toy with the future of your son.'

"Well she, being a woman, began to cry of course, calling me a fool. Nevertheless, the affair dissolved and I don't regret it. I acted nobly. For the sake of my own blind passion I didn't sacrifice the youthful organism of a child.

"I took myself completely in hand. I gave her a day to calm down, then another, then I went to explain myself precisely.

"Of course, the woman could not comprehend it. She persisted: 'You fool, you fool.' Completely unfounded.

"So that's how the affair ended. And I can say I'm proud of my behavior. I forgot about it rather quickly, because in general I consider the harboring of memories unnecessary. What good are they? You can't pawn them or anything.

"Well, having thought the situation over, I was still determined to get married. Only not to a Russian—no way! You have to be logical about this. Where are we living? I ask you frankly—where? In France. And since we live in France, it's necessary to marry a French woman. So I began to look for one.

"I have a certain French friend here, Monsieur Emelian. He's not pure French, but he's lived here a long time and he knows all the customs.

"Well, this monsieur introduced me to a certain young lady. She works at the post office. Sweet. I just looked at her, you know, and oh! Her figure's really great. Tall and thin. And her dress fits her like it's poured on.

"Uh-oh, I think I'm gonna be in hot water!

" 'No,' I told my friend, 'this one doesn't suit me. I like her, I haven't a thing against her, but you have to be logical. Such a thin, well-built creature will always be able to buy inexpensive dresses—maybe for seventy-five francs. But once she buys a dress, there'll be no keeping her home any more. She'll have to go out dancing. And what's the good in that? Is that what I'm marrying for, so that my wife will go out dancing? No, I said, find me a model of a different series. More thickset. And you can imagine—she was quickly found. Not a large model, really, but a stocky one, with enough fat on her bones so you don't have to buy any, as they say. But in general, she wasn't bad-looking, and she worked. Now don't think that she's some kind of an ox. No, she has little curls, and waves, and everything that the thin ones have. Only, of course, you can't find ready-made dresses for her.

"Having thought it all over, I revealed to her what was to be done under the circumstances, and we were off to the mayor.

"Well, after about a month, she asked me for a new dress. She asked for a new dress, and I very willingly said: 'Of course! Will you buy a ready-made one?'

"She blushed slightly and answered offhandedly: 'I don't like ready-made dresses. They don't fit me well. I'd rather you bought me some blue material and took it to a seamstress.'

"So I very readily kissed her and went off to buy some material. And as if by mistake I bought the most ill-suited color. Something like dun, like you find in horses.

"She was a little confused, but she thanked me anyway. She didn't have any choice—it was the first gift. It's too easy to scare future gifts away. She, too, understands the importance of strategy.

"Well, I felt very happy about everything and recommended a Russian seamstress to her. I've known this seamstress for a long time. She fleeces worse than a Frenchwoman and sews so badly that you just spit and fume. She sewed one client's collar to his sleeve, and still she argued. So this same *couturière* sewed a dress for my lady. Well, it was so funny that you wouldn't have to go to the theater to laugh. She was a dun-colored heifer, nothing more! She'd already tried to cry, the poor thing, and to alter it, and to dye it—nothing helped. The dress hangs just like that on a nail even now, and my wife sits at home. She's French, she understands that you can't have a dress made every month. So we live a quiet family life. I'm very content. And why? Because I'm logical.

"I even taught her to cook stuffed cabbage rolls.

"Happiness isn't just placed into your hands. You have to know how to lay your hands on it. And even though everyone would like to, not everyone can. You have to be logical!"

The Magpie

She wore an imbecilic and anxious look.

Her manner was fussy. She was always muttering and jostling things.

She always dressed entirely in black and white—but right now this combination was in vogue.

Her nose was long. Her eyes were round, discontented and stupid.

Don't look for any women you know who might fit this description, though. You won't find them. That is, if you do find them, they're not the one we're talking about. Because we're talking about a bird, a magpie.

This magpie lived in Paris, on Cretelle Street, across from the hospital garden.

Here's how we got to know her:

One day we happened to be passing the hospital garden, out walking our dog. Suddenly we saw a bird shuffling along the sidewalk. It looked disgruntled and not afraid of us at all.

Our dog began to bark at it, but the bird didn't bat an eye. On the contrary, it began to squawk angrily, as if cursing, and advanced on the dog sideways.

"What an amazing thing!"

"It must be tame."

Just then a woman's head poked itself out of the ground floor window and called: "Kiki!"

This "Kiki" was clearly addressed to the magpie. (Everything that's not a horse or a cow is "Kiki" to the French. "Kiki" is a rabbit, a canary, a monkey, a turtle, a hippopotamus in the zoo, even one's own granddaughter.) So the magpie was "Kiki", and it was obviously tame.

We wanted to find out more.

It turns out we were right. Kiki was tame. As well as famous along the whole block.

That's how the ice was first broken. And from then on we began to run into the magpie on her street. She was always angry and preoccupied with some complicated, urgent matters, and it was obvious that these matters were not going well.

Then one day the magpie disappeared. We no longer met her on the street. Maybe she was sick?

It was somehow awkward to make inquiries. It seemed as though questions were not fitting. An intrusion into private life.

God knows why the bird no longer strolled around the neighborhood. In civilized countries, mutual acquaintances aren't supposed to give out the addresses of their friends, even if you ask about them. God knows what could happen. Maybe it's you they're hiding from. In civilized countries, private life is sacred.

"Why isn't the magpie strolling around anymore?"

"What's it to you? Don't be so nosy."

So we had to suppress our mutual curiosity, and little by little the magpie diminished in our memory.

But one fine day, as we were walking along that same magpie street, we overheard a conversation. A passerby was talking with that same woman's head, which had poked out of the ground floor window and called the magpie "Kiki."

"Why don't we ever see your magpie any more?" asked the passerby.

"Oh, she's terribly busy," answered the head. "She's begun building a nest and is looking for a husband."

We couldn't resist any longer: "Where is her nest? You'll forgive us for asking. It's not just idle curiosity. We're like old friends. We met her often . . . maybe she needs something?"

"Just turn around," the woman's head directed us. "See the large tree beyond the fence? Her nest is in it way up high. It's a marvellous nest! Luxurious. She's already lugged all sorts of stuff up there. My daughter's ribbon disappeared. We looked all over for it—ran our legs off—and then Madame Racoux says she saw that magpie carting it off. Julie's sports pin disappeared, Micheline's spoon. My husband wanted to climb up to the nest and have a look, feel around in it, but it's very high up, a difficult climb. She's fixed everything up there quite splendidly. Now she's sitting and waiting for a husband. Only you don't see any magpies around here, just sparrows. And she's not at all suitable for a sparrow."

"In Medon there are tons of magpies," the passerby interjected.

"Yes, so they tell me. But how can we let them know about her? They never fly over this way."

"She could fly over there herself."

"But she doesn't know they're there."

"I've heard that there are talking magpies. If you'd only taught her to talk, you could explain to her about Medon."

"It's too late to teach her now. It's not talking she's interested in now."

"Well, maybe some bird will turn up here yet. Birds do fly, you know. One of them will see her from the air and spread the news."

"If a magpie sees her, that is. They're so talkative. It's not for nothing that we say, 'chatter like a magpie.' "

Another month or so passed. Once again we found ourselves on that street. Once again the woman's head was sticking out of the window.

This time, like kin already united by common magpie interests, we got right down to business: "*Bonjour, bonjour*, how is she? Did she find a husband?"

The head shook dejectedly. "Oh, if you only knew! She waited and waited and decided that her nest wasn't magnificent enough. Just imagine, she abandoned it and started to build a new one! A huge one. Really, as if she were expecting an eagle! My heart aches for her. But how can you explain to her that that's not the problem?"

"If only she'd been taught to speak in time!"

"Well, who could have known?"

Once again a rather long time passed before we had a conversation with the woman's head. "What's new?"

"Real trouble. What a tale it's turned out to be! She built a nest that amazed everyone. Not just a bird—an aviator could have settled down there. The magpie waited and waited, but nothing came of it. So she decided to say to hell with a lawful union and manage by her own means. She lay eggs—unfertilized ones—and now she's just sitting and brooding. She's been sitting two months already. She's grown thin and mangy—just a nose and eyes. She even lost her tail. She flies off for a minute, flies around the nest three times—apparently for exercise—and then settles down again."

"What can we do? She'll kill herself that way."

"Yes, everyone on the block is concerned."

"Shouldn't we let some sort of society know?"

"The Salvation Army?"

"Don't be silly! The Animal Shelter."

"But a magpie isn't technically an animal."

"So in your opinion, if she's not an animal, you can let her die?"

"She'd be better off settling in Medon, the little fool."

"Let's not return to that old question every time! It's far simpler to buy a magpie in a pet shop and bring it here, than to drag a woman to Medon."

"What woman? You're mixing things up!"

"I meant to say 'magpie.'"

"Buy one in a store! That's our nice way of putting everything into material terms! The most sacred thing in the world is mother love, and man goes and pokes his nose into it with his monetary power. It's vile!" the old woman's head bobbed angrily.

"I beg you not to reproach me. You know, she simply started in the wrong order. First you have to find a suitor—only then can you decorate the apartment."

"How you love to vulgarize everything!" the old woman's head hissed.

"Watch yourself! I'll ask you to keep your . . ."

"Surely you can see it's unpleasant for me when you talk about her like that!" the head cried.

"What exactly did I say? I can't even talk about a magpie in normal language! What a nightmare!"

"Hey, calm down!" someone interjected. "You'll end up quarreling!"

"So we'll quarrel! When someone is struggling for the ideals of motherhood, ridicule is completely out of place."

"We still have to prove that ideals are involved here. In my opinion, the magpie's an old hag who's ready to hang on everyone's neck, like a lunatic. We've all known people like that before. No need to go far—you've probably heard about our Lukiya Tarasovna, Madame Kudyselo? She lives in our hotel. What, you haven't heard about her? She keeps boarders. Such a resourceful woman. Two married sons, one grandson. Well, last year this lady decided to change her fate. That is, to get married. We all simply gasped. Between you and me, her appearance isn't exactly suited to such plans. Her shoulders are wide and thick and her legs—it's as if she doesn't have any legs at all. When she sits, her knees disappear somewhere beneath her stomach. And on top of that, she has no neck whatsoever, just a furrow, and that's it. This lady's voice is very peculiar. Not that it's unpleasant, but in our present émigré life, it's no longer appropriate. It reminds you of the old women calling back and forth to each other across the fences back home in the Ukraine. That's the kind of sound it has, the volume, the inflection. Can you imagine it? And on top of all that, this Lukiya Tarasovna has a snub nose, her eyes are as white as raw fish, and there's a bald spot on her head.

"When she told us of her plan, we couldn't even laugh, we just said: 'Maybe you should consider your age. Your grandson might be offended.'

"But she just snorted in reply. 'I'm surprised at your ignorance,' she said. 'Back in Russia, a woman is already considered an old lady by the time she hits forty. But here, my dears, it's different. Here a woman just begins to bloom again at fifty. Someone once took me to a theater here, they call it a music hall. There was an old lady there, about seventy, I'd say, the queen of the whole performance. She brought six gorgeous fellows out onto the stage and placed them in a row. Then they threw this old lady back and forth through the air for large sums of money. They just grabbed her by the legs and hup! I

The Magpie

squealed every time. That's the way things are here, and you tell me it's too late for me to get married.'

"Well, Madame Kudyselo put an ad in a magazine: 'Melancholy blonde, able to cook a little, languishes for the ideal and wants to enter into serious correspondence with thirty-three-year-old brunet. Size no object.'

"And what do you think? She received a letter from Grenoble: 'Idealist, disappointed in life, awaits his dream. Has a small but steady income.'

"So she sent him an old photograph, he sent her money for the trip, and our lady set off for Grenoble.

"She arrived at the station and couldn't find anyone resembling him there. There was only a plump old man wandering around peeking out from under his hat at all the young ladies. Madame Kudyselo peered at the old man and saw, sticking out of his pocket, the same magazine where she'd placed her ad. It took her breath away. She began to yell in her loud voice, like an old woman across a fence: 'Oy, can you really be the idealist? Oy, baldie!'

"His eyes popped open wide, and how he began to cluck!

"'Cluck-cluck-cluck! So this is you? What kind of picture did you send me? From before the Japanese War of '05?'

"But Madame Kudyselo would not give in to insult: 'Well, what was I supposed to send you? An i.d. with a crooked snout, squint-eyes and three noses? You're a lousy idealist—with pretensions, no less!'

"She went on to accuse him of being a petty official, he called her an old blob of dough. Still, he had to buy her a return ticket, as well as a beer in the buffet, because she berated him so much. So she came back by return train."

The old woman's head finally had a chance to speak. "These stories of yours about people I don't know are fine and dandy. As a poet once expressed it: 'Where there are waves, there are storms; where there are people, there are passions.' But what about the magpie?"

"Things are more complicated with a magpie. No poet ever immortalized a magpie. A magpie suffers deeply, you know. You can't get off with just buying her a beer . . ."

How wise Mother Nature is! When you really think about it, it makes you sick.

Secret Hiding Places Revealed

Our conversation turned to finding money on the street and what happens afterwards.

We discussed how the laws treat the finder in different countries. In Persia, the finder becomes the victim, because he is taken to the police station, and once a person lands in a Persian police station, he's always beaten before interrogation—just for the record.

We recalled that even in Russia the procedure was something like that. Of course, they didn't actually beat you at the police station, but they did afford you quite a few unpleasantries.

We remembered the story of a certain gentleman who'd dropped his wallet. Just as he bent down to pick it up, someone's hand pulled the wallet right out from under his nose. The owner of the hand, a shady character, stated in a business-like way: "I'm sorry, but *I* found this wallet."

"What do you mean, *you* found it," the gentleman yelled, "when it's my wallet and I can prove it!"

"If it's yours, it's yours," the character calmly agreed. "But since I found it, one-sixth of it belongs to me. And I have witnesses. So let's go to the police station, if you don't mind."

One of his witnesses appeared—not exactly a sterling character, either.

They dragged the loser to the police station.

The officer listened to the finder and his witness and counted the money in the wallet: sixty rubles. "Well now," he says to the man who lost his wallet. "You have to give thirty rubles to the finder, and thirty to the witness, and ten to me for drawing up the statement."

"I beg your pardon!" the loser pleaded. "Why so much? I lost a total of sixty rubles, but you've calculated a debt of seventy."

The officer replied, "You must have lost too little, then."

Many stories are told about finds and their consequences, but they all more or less resemble each other. However, we did recall one which stands out from the others, even though it is similar to a degree. It stands out because of its exceptional ending, which reveals that the secret hiding places of the human soul are so astounding that perhaps it would be better not to disclose them at all.

****

The beginning of the story is most banal.

Once upon a time there were two ladies. Both were young and attractive. Both had lost their husbands in the whirlpool of current events. They differed from each other mainly in that one was well-to-do, the other decidedly poor. This situation was apparently firmly fixed for both of them: the rich lady was a practical woman who never let go of her own property while managing to keep a sharp eye on the the property of others; but the poor one was a bungler, undone by life, who although dissatisfied with her modest lot, had resigned herself with a sigh.

These ladies had known each other for a long time, even before fate had defined their material positions so sharply. They had been friendly at first; then they saw each other only occasionally, and no longer as equals, because the elegant lady with plucked brows and a *permanente mise en pli* refused to consider herself on the same intellectual level with a creature wearing a dress of imitation silk, *garanti-lavable*, which cost eighty-nine francs ninety centimes, a creature with an unshaven neck and unplucked brows, as unimproved as when her mother bore her. Towards such a creature one only can be condescending. One can stand her, pity her, love—yes, even love her—but of course one can never consider her an equal.

One day these two ladies (for the sake of convenience let's call them Marivanova—the rich one—and Kolayeva—the poor one) were walking along on some sort of ladies' business. Whether the poor one suggested to the rich one to look at some bargain, or whether the rich one took the poor one to show her some Paris model for copying, I don't know—it's not important to our story in any case. Only the fact that they were walking along together has significance.

As they were walking along, the poor one suddenly spied a wallet lying on the sidewalk, not far from the store "Printemps."

"Look, Zhenichka, a wallet."

The rich one replied, "We'd better pick it up."

As the poor one stooped to get it, the rich one said: "Give it to me—you don't know how to handle money." And she took the wallet.

The two women looked inside and discovered forty-two thousand francs. They gasped.

"We'd better run right to the police station!" exclaimed the poor one.

"Whatever for?" The rich one was surprised. "Some ne'er-do-well loses his money like this, and we're supposed to give it back? No, we'll teach him a lesson. He won't be so careless again!"

But the poor one, impractical person that she was, was indignant.

"We can't just take other people's money! Especially since there's a calling card in the wallet, so we know who the owner is. That would be robbery!"

They argued for a long time until the poor one, in her nobility, threatened to go to a gendarme and tell him everything.

So the rich one decided to go straight to the owner and return his money in person. The poor one agreed, and they set off.

They arrived at a large apartment. A servant greeted them. He asked them to come in and went to announce their arrival.

The rich one said to the poor one: "You wait in the hall. The devil knows how you're dressed—you'll embarrass me."

So the rich one went in to see the host, a most attractive gentleman: elegant, with grey temples, platinum teeth, a manicure, and smelling of expensive cigars. He received her cordially, listened to her story, delightedly accepted his wallet, and after counting the money, abandoned himself to grateful ecstasy. Then he asked: "But where is your friend? After all, you say that there were two of you."

"She's waiting in the hall," Marivanova said.

"Oh no, how can that be!"

The gentleman ran into the hall and found the embarrassed Kolayeva. He seated her, thanked her, and invited them both out to a restaurant that evening. Later they all met again. And even though he didn't give them a penny for finding his wallet, neither felt offended because both of them liked him very much. He took them for drives, he treated them, and even if he had hinted at some kind of reward, he would only have succeeded in embarrassing his new friends.

One day in conversation the details of the find were made clear. The poor one blurted out that it was she who had insisted that the money be returned to its owner. In saying this she didn't in the least mean to slander the rich one. She emphasized that the idea of giving the find to the owner in person came to the rich one, but nevertheless the owner (let's simply call him the Frenchman, for convenience's sake) understood that he had received his money thanks only to Kolayeva's persistent honesty. Aware besides that she was as poor as a rat and worked like an ox, and comparing these two creatures, so different in their sizes and their strengths, he was imbued with such tenderness for the noble Slavic soul of Kolayeva that he not only fell head over heels in love with her, but even proposed to her without considering all the (so-called) vile propositions.

The rich one was very hurt by his choice, of course, but what could she do? She had to resign herself to it. And since the poor one had not only become equal to her in rank, but was even one up on her (the rich one had a Citroën, the poor one, a Buick; the rich one—three rooms, the poor one—six; the rich one—the corner hairdresser, the poor one—Antoine), it was now possible to enter into genuine friendship with her.

The Frenchman was in a state of bliss. He studied his Slavic soul, but... then the trouble began. The Frenchman began to look closely at things.

"Why are three thousand francs missing? Where are they?"

"Gone to charity."

"Where's the picture that was hanging in the dining room—the one of the rabbits with the raspberries?"

"I donated it to the lottery."

"Who is that fool who's always sitting in the linen closet, eating something?"

"She's a good woman whose own children chased her out because of her bad character. Where else can she go?"

Eventually these circumstances began to displease the Frenchman.

"Darling!" the former poor one said in answer to his reproaches. "Darling! Wasn't it for my tender and pure soul that you fell in love with me? Am I not behaving as I behaved before? Look, the picture that was hanging in the dining room was won in the lottery. Doesn't it follow then that we should donate it for the lottery's benefit? And you yourself said that the three thousand francs fell to you by chance. Doesn't it follow..."

"Nothing follows from anything else!" the Frenchman snapped.

"But why then before..."

"Before I liked it that you decided to give back the money belonging to me. But now that you're giving my money to others, I don't like it at all. This side of the Slavic soul definitely repulses me. Go take a lesson from your friend, Madame Marivanova. Now there's a woman who understands the value of money. She's practical and pleasant besides."

Jealousy flared up in the former poor one's heart.

"Maybe she is pleasant," she said in a trembling voice, "but she borrowed my pearls for one day and hasn't returned them for three months. I know she wants to keep them for good. And you're telling me that's *practical*?"

"If there's anything distasteful in that story," her husband answered disdainfully, "it's your negligence. Madame Marivanova understands the value of things, she treasures them, and in general she possesses the attributes of a good wife. Your character is not well suited to a wife."

"Do you approve of the fact that she wanted to keep other people's money for herself?"

"If I had been her husband then, I would have found her behavior both pleasant and useful."

At this point the former poor one began to cry.

The further course of their conversation is not known. All we do know is that the Frenchman divorced the former poor one and married the former rich one, Madame Marivanova.

And that's the uncommon ending to this common story.

A Bright Life

The world was created in five days.

"And God saw that it was good," the Bible says.

He saw that it was good, so He created man.

"Whatever for?" you may ask.

Who knows?

Nevertheless, He created him. And that's how it all began. God saw that it was good, but Man saw that it was not so good. Man immediately began to complain: this is bad, that's wrong, why are there commandments, why prohibitions?

And then there's that sad story everyone knows about the apple. Man ate the apple, but the blame fell on the snake. The snake put me up to it, he says. (That's human nature: a child plays a trick on his friend, and the friend is blamed when they get into trouble.)

However, it's not the fate of Man that interests us right now, merely the question: Why was he created? Maybe because the universe, like every artistic creation, was in need of criticism?

Of course, not everything in this universe is perfect. There's a lot of nonsense in it. For example, why do twelve different varieties of meadow grass exist, and all for no reason? Just so a cow can come plodding along and indiscriminately gobble up all twelve with her wide tongue?

And what does Man need an appendix for? To make work for idle surgeons' hands?

"Tut, tut, your reasoning is frivolous," they say. "Our worm-shaped appendix testifies to the fact that Man once . . ."

I don't remember what it testifies to—probably something highly unflattering, like belonging to a certain species of ape or to some Southeast Asian variety of cuttlefish. It would be better not to testify at all. Worm-shaped? Ugh! But still, in His infinite wisdom, God created the appendix.

Besides the gift of criticism, Man was also given the gift of imagination. Criticism judges; imagination concocts. Imagination cannot, of course, improve upon something factual. And everything factual is for the most part so boring and imperfect that it's often unpleasant to accept it for what it is—something artistically unsuccessful.

There are people in the world who cannot accept these mundane facts, who cannot accept them and do not want to reckon with them. In their opinion, a fact can be mistaken, just as Man can be.

And these people, not perceiving everyday life as aesthetic, must improve upon it with their imaginations (an organ certainly created in the same spirit as the appendix), and a new everyday life lives in them, ever expanding in its already improved form.

In common parlance this ability is simply called lying.

****

The preceding merely introduces our story about Valentina Petrovna. The story is short, encompassing in all only one day in her life, a life rich in events.

Valentina Petrovna lives like all of us do, with ups and downs. That's on the outside. But in fact her life is rich in content, kaleidoscopic and varied.

The externals of her life go like this: she is fifty-five years old (this does relate to the externals, you know), badly dressed in secondhand clothes, with multicolored hair and a wrinkled face, but the expression in her eyes is inspired.

She lives in a room at the widow Parfyonova's, who knits sweaters to sell. She doesn't pay too regularly for her room, but from her point of view, it's nonsense to do so. (Parfyonova does not agree with this outlook, but she's decided to put up with it for the time being.) Valentina Petrovna's occupation is selling Parfyonova's sweaters, sewing wallets, and so on—whatever crops up. Sometimes, when there is a lot of work, she sits at home for three or four days in a row without leaving the house, but—she can't complain—she absorbs a mass of impressions all the same.

"The mailman came while you were out," she says to Parfyonova. "I don't know if that man has ever loved, but I read in his energetic face great selflessness and readiness to struggle for personal happiness, qualities I have rarely ever met with. I thought about him for a long time, and his memory will probably be deeply engraved on my soul for the rest of my life."

Or:

"The delivery man brought the coal while you were out. You know, I'm struck by the extraordinarily rhythmic movements of his body. I sense an exceptionally talented nature in him, and if he had followed a different path in life, who knows, maybe he would have become a second Van Dyke."

If Valentina Petrovna went outside, she had only to go as far as the corner bakery for her life to be filled with impressions enough for two days.

She would unfailingly meet some girl with Italian eyes, an urchin (but from high society, of course), or she'd meet some kid, some grocer's daughter, who had obviously been stolen as a child from her noble parents, as evidenced by her unusually aristocratic nose.

She would meet a man in the dairy whom she didn't know at all. He would look at her as if he wanted to say: "Your soul is not hidden to me. You are tender and lonely, and I understand the beauty of your sadness."

"Where do you come up with all this?" the widow Parfyonova would ask, amazed.

If Valentina Petrovna happened to spend an evening visiting, her stories would last for a month. What just one trip was worth!

"Yesterday on the trolley there was a military man, as far as I can judge by the precision of his bearing. He looked at me so strangely . . ." And so on and so forth.

"Amazing!" said Parfyonova. "You always manage to pick someone up! Here I take the trolley every day, and except for fleas, I can't pick up anything.

The day our story begins, Valentina Petrovna was taking a sweater to the Popovs. The Popovs had company, and she was invited to drink a cup of tea with them. They were talking about a certain Bykov, who was unfaithful to his wife.

"She'll get over it soon," someone interjected. "She seems to have fallen for some French artist."

"I don't doubt it," someone else observed. "She's such an insipid person."

After this comment Valentina Petrovna took her leave and went by trolley to the Shurins.

A lot of people were crowded into the trolley car. She had to stand. Then one gentleman got up and offered her his seat.

The man was young and simply dressed, wearing a thick knitted muffler and holding two storebought packages wrapped in paper.

Valentina Petrovna, agitated and confused, examined him closely.

"Simple, yet elegant," she thought. "A knight. Just the type women like. If that poor Bykova they were just talking about met a man like him along her way, he would console her. He is a knight. But maybe—and there's nothing surprising in this supposition— maybe he's that very Frenchman she's fallen for! But I don't want to stand in her way. That would be dreadful. I can step aside. I'll go up to him right now and say: 'I know that you're an artist, that poor Bykova loves you, I'll get out of the picture.' 'I'll get out of the picture.' I'll say that and jump down from the trolley platform, and the quiet twilight of the huge city will swallow my steps."

"Rue Lurmel," the conductor cried.

Valentina Petrovna jumped up. This was her stop—the Shurins lived on Lurmel.

Oh horror, oh happiness, *he* got off too! He was following her, her!

With a loudly beating heart she slackened her pace and turned around. No. He had turned toward the boulevard. But they would meet again. It was destined.

Everyone at the Shurins was surprised at her pallor. And she could not keep quiet.

"Something very strange just happened. More fantastic than any novel I've ever read," she recounted. "You know me, I'm not a flirt or a beauty. I behave simply, I dress modestly. So I don't know, I don't understand, how to explain the strange attention with which I'm surrounded in life. Why you like me, why Parfyonova adores me—this I can understand. But why completely strange people are so drawn to me—this simply frightens me sometimes. I assure you—it doesn't flatter me. I don't need anyone or anything. A pair of doves on a window sill, a half-wilted rose in a vase, a book of my favorite poetry in my lap, a light breeze rustling my curls—that's everything I need. So why this whirlwind of passion? Why these unnecessary appeals? I don't want them now and never have. And now look—a drama... You, my friends, I'll tell you the whole truth. That good-for-nothing Bykov abandoned his wife. She, the poor sufferer, fell in love with a French artist. It would seem that fate itself was laughing at her. The artist is a knight, he's nobility in a woolen muffler. He can give her happiness. But then—our fatal meeting... It's all the same, how and where. I swear to you—I'm not guilty. I didn't lure him away. And I don't love him. I don't want to unite my life—which even without this passion is so stormy—with his spectral existence. What can I do? I have decided to go away before it's too late. Money is no problem. I can always obtain two or three thousand. People I'm dear to will always come to my aid. It will be hard for you to lose me, I know. Parfyonova, too. And many others. I'll live somehow... but all of you—what will become of you?"

At that moment the doorbell rang.

Valentina Petrovna, sitting by the door to the hall, jumped up to let Shurin pass and went together with him into the hall. He opened the door.

"Oh, my God!"

The gentleman from the trolley, the one in the thick woolen muffler... Valentina Petrovna swayed and clutched at her breast with both hands.

"*Livraison!*" said the gentleman from the trolley, holding out a package.

"Liza! They've sent the lamp," Shurin called to his wife. "Give the delivery boy a franc for tea."

Valentina Petrovna leaned against the door frame so she wouldn't fall.

She saw Liza Shurin give the man in the muffler a franc for tea, and he said, "*Merci, Madame,*" and slammed the door behind him.

She didn't want to tell the Shurins everything right away. She wanted, and rightly so, to think everything over, to understand—how did the mad artist think that whole scheme up and carry it out?

And in the evening or the next morning she would tell the whole fantastic story to the widow Parfyonova, after getting her word, of course, that she wouldn't tell anyone.

"How interesting, complicated, and rich my life is! How awesome and how bright!"

Scoundrels

How old is she?

She's about fifty or fifty-five, something like that. Red hair, tightly curled, like the mane of an Assyrian lion. Round cheeks the color of blotting paper, which quiver slightly when she gets angry. Brushed lashes, plucked brows, dresses with pleats, lace, bows and frills. In short, the woman takes care of herself and knows what she's worth.

Yes, she knows what she's worth and therefore it's impossible to argue with her.

She speaks authoritatively, brushing objections aside with her hand: "Forget it!" Or: "Oh, come on!"

It's not hard for her to change your opinions. After all, she's the one who's always right.

Her name is Alevtina Petrovna.

"Darling," says Alevtina Petrovna. "Have you heard that Shura's getting married?"

"So let her!"

"What do you mean, 'let her'! To get married means to marry a man! A scoundrel!"

"Why do you say 'scoundrel'?"

"Oh, come on! Have you ever met a man who wasn't a scoundrel? Have you ever met one who didn't betray his wife? I once knew an old lady, a woman of great experience. She always said, 'Alevtya, dearie, believe me—men are God's dogs.' She always called them that. She was a woman of great experience. She knew all about them."

"No doubt she had a whole pack of these dogs during her long life?"

"Well, yes, she probably had to suffer quite a bit, poor thing. 'Alevtya,' she'd say, 'darling, believe me—they all have nothing but females on their minds.' She understood everything. I think of her often... You know, sometimes you drop in to hear a lecture. Some public figure or bearded professor walks across the stage, hair like a cornshock. I look at him and I think: 'Go ahead and shuffle—you won't fool me. I know what's on your mind.' No, my dear, it wasn't for nothing that Pushkin wrote:

> 'Men roam the streets that way
> To seek an easy lay...'"

"What are you talking about? When did Pushkin ever write that?"

"He wrote it, he didn't consult us. But just think—Shura's young and pretty, and suddenly she's getting married. I told her mother: 'Quite frankly, your Shura's a fool.' But the mother, she says, 'Oh my, but he's so interesting and he has money and a good job.' So I said to her: 'Maybe he has a job, I won't argue. But as for his loving her—I'll tell you frankly—believe it or not, his relationship to her is pure pornography.' But do you think Shura and her mother are really capable of understanding? My God, how many dirty male tricks I've seen in my day! . . . Not long ago I stopped in at a cafe. I look—there's a familiar face at one of the tables. General Kukhormin. With a young girl. They sit and drink coffee. And he's chuckling, he's *bleating* at her! For shame! I couldn't even finish my ice cream. I left without paying, it was so repulsive to me. The next day I saw him at the Burlakovs'. I took him aside and said: 'I saw you yesterday. I won't tell Sofia Petrovna anything, of course, but to you I have to express my indignation.' And that scoundrel—can you imagine!—he began to defend himself!

"'Now look,' he says, 'there was nothing especially wrong with my behavior. Sometimes a man wants to cheer himself up a little. I deeply appreciate and respect Sofia Petrovna, but I don't have erotic feelings for her anymore.'

"Can you believe the swine? He doesn't have feelings! Towards the noblest of wives, who's given him the bloom of her life, sacrificed forty-five years for him, borne him eight children and been a model hostess (what pies!); who's constantly suffering from rheumatism, gout, sciatica, biliousness, scrofula, jaundice, an adipose heart, legs like logs—I saw them myself. For a woman like that he doesn't have erotic feelings, but for a painted slut he does! You can tell what a scoundrel he must be to go that far! I wanted to slap his face right then and there, but we were called to the table, so it was inconvenient.

"Oh, I could tell you a lot about these scoundrels!

"For instance, a certain landowner, name of Kolyshev, a maniac, used to live in our town. What a snout he had!—the kind people call 'natural.' Pot-bellied, nose like a horn, mouth always gaping, tongue lolling out. Still, he would run after females for days on end. He'd go into a restaurant—four of them are already waiting for him. He'd go into a cafe—five of them are watching to see if he's on his way."

"Excuse me—but it sounds like the females were running after him, not the other way around!"

"Well, you know, it's possible to turn everything around. If that good-for-nothing asks, implores, and entreats them to come, then not every woman has the heart to spurn him.

Scoundrels

"Anyway, this same Snoutface latched onto one of our ladies. Polenka Okurko. Polenka wasn't bad-looking. She was a flighty little lady, she didn't hide it. She'd simply say: 'To hell with all that.' Polenka was sincere, a fresh soul.

"Well, that viper just hung on to her and told her that if she'd go abroad with him, he'd buy her all kinds of gifts, and if she'd be faithful to him for three months, he'd make out a will in her favor. He even hinted that he had heart trouble, so she'd know that his talk of a will wasn't an empty offer...

"Well, Polenka thought about it, consulted her hairdresser, and decided to go along with him. Three months isn't such a long time—it's possible to endure—and God willing, the travelling would exhaust him and the will would become valid...

"So she went.

"Well, it turned out that I was also going abroad at that time, to Venice. I stopped at a hotel there and just happened to look at the guest list where I saw 'Señor Kolyshev.' Aha, I thought, so here's where our friends are! Their room turned out to be on the same hall as mine.

"Well, the minute Polenka found out I was at the hotel she came running to me.

"Even though she was flighty, I sympathized with her greatly. Why not? A single woman makes ends meet as best she can. And Polenka's sincere, a simple soul.

"I asked her how she was feeling.

"'I really like being abroad. Everyone here is so sweet, they're all so clean, they flutter their lashes in a special way, not like Russians. And yesterday this very brown man arrived, almost a black. Well, he was so interesting that I stared right at him, my mouth gaping, and I didn't know what to do. I don't know how to smile at a black man so that he'll understand the Russian soul.'

"And did your monster behave himself decently?" I asked.

"'No,' she says, 'my monster is a real bastard. He vowed and swore and promised me the moon, but all I got of that moon was three pairs of stockings in Vienna and a clothesbrush and toothbrush in Trieste. For some reason or other he had a fit of generosity with brushes in Trieste—maybe on account of the heat. But that's all. He himself used the clothesbrush, and finally he took it back.'

"What a bastard!" I say. "Well, any news about the will?"

"'He keeps repeating that if I can last for three months, then everything will be mine. Only he's jealous. He spies, he doesn't even let me take a breath. I can't stand it anymore!'

"Well, I calmed her down as best I could. Three months, of course, is a long time, but four weeks had already flown by successfully.

" 'Even though he spies like the devil, he hasn't caught me yet,' she said.

" 'Was there anything to catch?' I asked.

" 'Well, you know,' she says, 'a bastard like that can turn anything around.'

"So we go on living at the same hotel but don't see each other too often. I have my own friends and, I confess, I didn't try too hard to see that snout-faced monster.

"One night I was just about to turn out the light, when suddenly the door burst open wide and Polenka flew in—wearing nothing but her underwear!

" 'What's going on? What happened?' I asked her.

"She was trembling.

" 'Hide me quickly! The scoundrel's looking for me! He'll kill me!'

" 'At least throw on a bathrobe,' I said. 'How could you run naked through the hall?'

" 'For Christ's sake, say that I've been here with you all evening... I was at the Arab's. My monster went out to a cafe. I told him I had a headache. Just think—never in my life have I had an affair with an Arab, and I probably never will again. Where could you ever find an Arab in Ryazan? This was such an opportunity, the chance of a lifetime! How could I let it slip by? That would be idiotic!'

" 'Of course it would be! And all for whom? Snoutface? Lie down on my bed,' I said. 'I'll cover for you.'

"A minute hadn't passed when boom-boom! Pounding at the door.

" 'Who's there?'

" 'Kolyshev. Is she in there?'

" 'Of course she's here,' I say. 'She took a bath and came over here to rest.'

" 'Swear that that's the truth,' he barked.

" 'You're an ill-bred boor!' I cried. 'How dare you burst into a room at night where respectable women are resting? Get out of here immediately or I'll call the concierge.'

"Then Polenka begged: 'Let me stay here till morning. He'll cool off in the meantime and then I'll be able to get out of this mess.'

"Well, the poor thing really did get out of that mess somehow.

"I left Venice a short time later, but heard that he caught her two other times. What a bastard! Polenka, of course, couldn't stand him any longer, so she ran off to Berlin with some character. She just up and left, it was no big deal. She was gone about two weeks. Meanwhile this Snoutface returned to our town, caught a cold, was sick all winter, and towards spring he died.

"But only after his death was all the baseness of his soul finally revealed. Imagine, the bastard didn't leave poor Polenka a penny. Literally not a penny. How do you like that?

"All those scoundrels are that way. All of them. Look here: when a woman falls in love, she immediately begins to think—what can I give the object of my affections? A cigarette case, a tie—or maybe I should embroider him something? But a man, if he takes an interest in your beauty, he immediately wants something as a 'memento,' the scoundrel. And what kind of memento does he need when he's under your nose morning till night? When would he have a chance to forget you? A certain character once courted me for an hour and a half, and in that time he'd already managed to filch my handkerchief. He grabbed it, sniff-sniffed it, and right into his pocket it went. How seductive he thought he was! And I had only half a dozen of those handkerchiefs with lace. He broke the set.

"When my friend Larisa got married, she found thirty-two women's handkerchiefs in her husband's desk, stuck in between his tax sheets. The fool was even proud of him: 'My husband was a Don Juan.'

" 'As far as I'm concerned,' I said, 'you'd be better off finding out some details. Maybe he wasn't a Don Juan, but a burglar.'

"And do you know, she was offended! Well, God be with her. I'm not angry, I feel sorry for her. She's had reason to cry buckets of tears with that scoundrel. As soon as her children began to grow older, she hired a Russian-German governess to teach them French. Just like they do in good homes. Well, she kept hearing her husband declaiming something:

'I love you, creation of Peter!'*

'It's from the classics,' he said.

"And his wife, she found his interest in poetry pleasing, of course. Only suddenly it hit her like a log in the forehead. The governess's name was Anna Petrovna!** There's your creation of Peter for you! And did she kick the governess out? Of course she did! The scoundrel feigned surprise. He laughed. As if that cost him a lot! Those scoundrels can play out comedies we would never even dream

---

*The opening line of Pushkin's famous poem "The Bronze Horseman." (Trans.)

**Russians, besides having first names, are given patronymics formed from the father's first name. Petrovna, as in Anna Petrovna, designates Anna as a daughter of Peter. So by extension she is a "creation of Peter." (Trans.)

of. They can even die out of spite. As God is my witness, I swear to you!

"Do you remember Anyuta Latuzina? What, you didn't know her? Impossible! You, from the same town... Well, Anyuta was an ill-fated woman. Now there was a martyr! Her husband, you see, was an engineer. For days on end he would bury his nose in blueprints, and you could beat your head against the wall for all he cared. He had tuberculosis. His wife worked like a fish beats against ice: it was always 'Run to the store,' 'Order dinner,' 'Entertain guests.' While he sits and calculates bridges. How do you like that? Then one early spring day he collapsed entirely. Anyuta, of course, felt nervous and angry. It's completely natural. She suggested we go together to Abbatsia, where her papa was taking a cure for the gout. He was supposed to have been quite a character in his day—it wasn't for nothing that his wife ran away from him, making off with their savings. Anyway, Anyuta respected him, probably because of his age. Well, I thought, why not go on an outing? We were eager to go. Anyuta's daughters stayed home with their father. They were already about fifteen and sixteen, and a pretty young woman can't cart such little calves along with her. But her six-year-old son, Volodyushka, she took along.

"We arrived in Abbatsia. Such beauty, the sea! You don't have to die to see Paradise. Papa wasn't a bad old codger—grey eyebrows, always eating something. The doctor put him on a diet, so he ate two dinners, one normal and one dietetic. 'This way,' he said, 'I'm still getting better, even if it's only halfway.' No, he wasn't a bad fellow. And his daughter loved him. Of course, he did have some money. It's easier to love a parent if he has money. It's more natural. Anyway, we're living there, getting along, when suddenly out of the blue a squall rolls in. To make a long story short, our Anyuta fell in love with a coachman. He was a big, healthy young fellow. Swiss. He had come just for the summer, to drive tourists to Montenegro. Ruddy as the devil. And Anyuta fell for him like it was her first love, like an adolescent. She behaved scandalously, jealously. For days on end she rode with him so that he didn't dare take others. She bought him gifts—a whip with a silver handle, a white leather jacket embroidered in silk. Such beauty! Such scandal! But what can you do? And how can you judge this, her first bright feeling?

"Well, the coachman wasn't so bad himself. He met her as often as he could. But you have to realize that four horses—that's a whole stable. You have to clean them and feed them, water them and harness them, and then feed them all over again. But the real problem was that our Anyuta didn't know ahh, ooh or cock-a-doodle-do in Swiss. And the coachman just happened to come from a canton where cretins live and the pronunciation is very difficult. A word in his dialect might sound like German, but it would have the opposite meaning. And besides, Anyuta wasn't any too quick with languages.

" 'How do you carry on conversations with him?' I asked.

" 'That's the problem!' she says. 'Mainly I use horse words—Giddyup and Stop! It's very difficult for complicated emotions.'

"She bought him a pair of boots with leggings. I began to give her valerian.

"Well, as luck would have it, the new tourists were beginning to arrive then, and of course they hired the coachman to take them around. The hotel had a car, but everyone preferred the carriage—it's more pleasant and much better for admiring the scenery.

"Well, our Anyuta was furious. She was still a little afraid of her Papenka, otherwise I really don't know what would have happened.

"Papenka, the old egotist, thought of no one but himself. He didn't even notice that his daughter was having these adventures.

"He couldn't leave the house, so he just hobbled about the room with his cane. He could barely bend his legs from the gout.

"One evening the old devil burst into Anyuta's room, just when the coachman was with her. Why couldn't the old wood-goblin have left her in peace? If you yourself can't sleep, at least don't bother others.

"Anyuta, poor thing, heard his footsteps in the hall. Naturally, she took fright and hid the coachman under her little boy's bed. The little boy was sleeping soundly, he didn't hear a thing.

"So Papenka comes into the room.

" 'Nyutochka,' he says, 'I wanted to take a peek at Volodka to see how he's sleeping.'

"You might think he found a sight! But no, the little boy was sleeping, just sleeping. As if there was anything to look at!

"So far, there wasn't any misfortune in his visit. The misfortune occurred when the old man's dog followed him in. It was some kind of mongrel, not a pure breed, not a fashionable dog in any way. And suddenly, you see, the hunting spirit awakened in this dog. It huffed up, its fur stood on end, and then it began barking under the bed. It barked so much that it wheezed.

"The old man became worried. 'What's going on here, darling?' he asked. 'Something is obviously wrong. Why is the dog barking like that under the bed? And why does the room smell like a stable? Has someone gotten in here?'

"Well, Anyuta kept her wits about her. 'This is very good and healthy for the child,' she said.

"But the old man feigned stupidity. 'What's healthy for the child?' he asked. 'That someone crawls under his bed?'

"Anyuta, naturally, was nervous. 'What kind of nonsense are you spouting? It's healthy not for someone to crawl under the bed, but for the room to smell like a stable. A normal animal smell is so beneficial to the lungs that sometimes it's purposely spread around rooms where there are children.'

"But the old man would not calm down. 'No, darling, something's wrong here. Why is the dog barking? Don't argue! Someone probably did get in here. We'd better call the servant.'

"Really, what an ass!

"Poor Anyuta was simply beside herself. Her only salvation was that the old man couldn't bend down to look under the bed.

" 'There's probably a rabbit under there,' she said. 'They gave the little boy a rabbit to play with today. I'd better chase the dog out, or it will tear the rabbit to pieces.'

"With difficulty she managed to throw them both out—the old man, and the dog.

"But then the coachman began to get capricious. 'Your dog will bite my nose off yet!' he cried.

"She barely managed to calm him down.

"Well, one day I saw Anyuta—what's the matter? She's not at all herself. She's downcast and angry.

" 'What a dreadful day!' she said. 'It's one dreadful thing after another. First, I got a letter from home—my husband is dying. Then the coachman tells me he lost his whip. And, as they say, trouble always comes in threes. Two pretty ladies arrived today. I didn't even have time to take precautions before they had driven off with the coachman till evening. I could just kill myself.'

"I asked her if it were true that her husband was so bad off.

" 'Ach,' she says, 'he's such a scoundrel—you don't know him. He's capable of getting sick out of spite, because he knows I'm so caught up in other things right now.'

"Well, somehow the old man got wind of this letter—they stick their noses everywhere!—and he ordered Anyuta to inquire about her husband by telegram.

"She inquired. Then she came to me all in tears.

" 'The answer came that if I want to find him alive, I have to leave immediately.'

"I looked at her, amazed. 'Nyutochka,' I say, 'why are you crying? He's been sick for a long time, you know. What good is such sentimentality?'

"But she began to cry even more. 'It's swinishness! It's the last word in boorishness: to die precisely now, when I can't leave the

Scoundrels

coachman alone because of those two hussies who are capable of I don't know what.'

"But the old man insisted she leave.

"So she left. For baggage she took only a small nail file. She didn't get any further than Venice before she returned.

" 'I can't go,' she said. 'My heart is breaking.'

"Everything turned out comparatively well, however. That very same day a telegram arrived saying that her tiresome engineer had given his soul up to God. So there was no longer any use in her leaving. The old man did spout some nonsense: 'It's indecent not to show up at the funeral,' he said. But poor Anyuta found enough strength in herself to defend her independence.

"Her situation really was alarming: the coachman was driving his good-for-nothings to the mountains and to the sea, just like the worst kind of scoundrel, and she's supposed to drop everything and leave! And for what? To oblige the posthumous egotism of her dead husband who—unwittingly perhaps—had nevertheless played a rather base role of late.

"The summer season ended and I left. I don't know how everything turned out after that. I didn't see Anyuta any more, she moved away somewhere.

"No, I didn't see Anyuta, but about ten years later, I heard about her by chance. Everything had turned out so surprisingly!

"I was living in Odessa then. One day I stopped in at my hairdresser's, and he told me the story:

" 'I had a new client today, a crazy woman. She kept waiting for some cavalier. She called him on the phone, she ran out to the street. She spilled a bottle of lotion, she knocked over a lamp, she almost set the place on fire—and then she suddenly leaped up and flew off somewhere, and here she forgot her wallet. I don't know what to do.'

"He showed me the wallet. I opened it, and there's a letter in it for—who do you think? Anna Ivanovna Latuzina—Anyuta, that's who! That's who was waiting for her cavalier, that's who called him on the telephone.

"My poor, poor sufferer! Some scoundrel is tearing your little dove heart to pieces again, I imagine. As if you haven't already suffered enough . . .

"And for what?"

A Virtuoso of Feeling

The most interesting thing about this man is the way he carries himself.

He's tall and thin; his bald eagle's head rests on a long neck. He walks with his elbows spread, rocking slightly at the waist, looking proudly all around. And since he is taller than almost everyone else, he looks to be astride a horse.

He lives on "crumbs" of some sort—but in spite of everything, not too badly. He rents a room with parlor and kitchen privileges and likes to prepare a special baked macaroni, which fires the imagination of the women he loves.

His last name is Gutbrecht.

Lizochka met him at a banquet benefiting "cultural undertakings and continuations."

He had evidently picked her out even before people were seated. She noticed the way he pranced past her three times on his invisible horse before digging in his spurs and galloping over to the toastmaster. He whispered something, all the while pointing at her, Lizochka. Then both of them—the horseman and the toastmaster—scrutinized the place cards arranged at the plates. They appeared to agree upon something, and Lizochka turned out to be Gutbrecht's dinner partner.

Gutbrecht lost no time in grabbing the bull by its horns. That is, he squeezed Lizochka's arm near the elbow and said to her with quiet reproach: "Darling! Well, why? Well, why not?"

In saying this, his eyes clouded over and became so moist that Lizochka took fright. But there was no reason to be frightened. This device of Gutbrecht's, renowned as "Number Five" ("I'm using 'Number Five' on her," Gutbrecht would say), was simply called "puppy-dog eyes" by his friends: "Look! Gut has already set his puppy-dog eyes in motion!" they'd titter.

As suddenly as he had grabbed Lizochka's arm, Gutbrecht let it go, saying in the calm tone of a refined man: "We'll start with the herring, of course."

But then he made his puppy-dog eyes again and whispered passionately, "God, how beautiful!"

Lizochka couldn't understand to whom this referred—to her or the herring—and out of confusion she couldn't eat.

Then a conversation began.

"When you and I go to Capri, I'll show you an unusual dog's cave," Gutbrecht cooed.

Lizochka trembled. Why should she go to Capri with him? How odd this gentleman was!

Diagonally across from her sat a tall, portly lady, of the caryatid type—beautiful and majestic.

Gutbrecht scornfully turned his bald head and turning it back just as scornfully, said, "Her little mug's not bad."

This "little mug" was so inappropriate to the majestic profile of the lady that Lizochka began to laugh.

Gutbrecht pursed his lips in a Cupid's bow and suddenly began to blink like an offended child. This he called "being a cutie."

"Baby! You're laughing at Vovochka!"

"Vovochka? Which Vovochka?" Lizochka was surprised.

"Me! I'm Vovochka!" Pouting his lips, the eagle's head played up to her.

Lizochka was amazed. "How strange you are! You're old, but you're acting like a baby."

"I'm only fifty!" Gutbrecht said sternly and blushed. He was insulted.

Lizochka was perplexed. "That's exactly what I'm saying—you're old!"

Gutbrecht was also perplexed. He had taken six years off his age and thought "fifty" sounded young.

"Darling," he said, suddenly changing to the familiar tone of address. "Darling, you're terribly provincial. If only I had more time, I'd concern myself with your upbringing."

"How dare you . . ." Lizochka was indignant.

But he interrupted her: "Hush! No one can hear us." And he added in a whisper: "I myself will protect you from scandal."

"If only this dinner would end!" thought Lizochka.

But then a speaker began his speech, and Gutbrecht quieted down.

"I live a strange but rich life!" he said when the speaker had finished. "I have devoted myself to the analysis of feminine love. It's complicated and painstaking work. I conduct experiments, I classify, I make conclusions. There's a lot that is unexpected and interesting. You know Anna Petrovna, of course? The wife of our well-known civic leader?"

"Of course I know her," Lizochka replied. "She's a very respectable lady."

Gutbrecht grinned and, spreading his elbows, pranced in place.

"Well, this very respectable lady is actually quite a little devil! A diabolical temperament! The other day she came to see me on business. I handed her the business papers and suddenly, not giving her a chance to realize what was happening, I grabbed her by the shoulders and fastened my lips onto hers. If only you'd seen what happened to her! She almost lost consciousness! Completely forgetting herself, she slapped my face and dashed out of the room. The next day I was supposed to drop in on her on business. She wouldn't receive me. You understand? She doesn't trust herself. You can't imagine how interesting such psychological experiments are! I'm no Don Juan, of course. No. I'm subtler. More inspired. I'm a virtuoso of feeling! Do you know Vera X? That proud, cold beauty?"

"Of course I know her. I've seen her several times."

"Well, not long ago I decided to awaken this marble Galatea. An opportunity soon presented itself, and I got my way."

"What are you saying!" Lizochka was amazed. "*Really*? Then why are you talking about it? How can you possibly talk about it?"

"I have no secrets from you. You know, I didn't fall for her for a single minute. It was a cold and cruel experiment. But it's so interesting that I want to tell you everything. There shouldn't be any secrets between us. So . . . It happened one evening at her house. I was invited to dinner for the first time. Among others, that lanky Stok or Strok—something like that—was there. They were talking as if he were still having an affair with Vera X. But that was just gossip. She is as cold as ice, but she woke up to life for one single moment. And it's this moment I want to tell you about. So, after dinner (there were about six of us, evidently all her close friends) we went into the semi-dark living room. I was near Vera on the couch. The conversation was general, not too interesting. Vera was cold and unapproachable. She was wearing an evening dress cut very low in back. Well, without interrupting the genteel conversation, I quietly but powerfully stretched out my arm and quickly slapped her several times on her bare back. If you only knew what happened to my Galatea then! How that cold marble suddenly came to life! Really, just think: a man at someone's house for the first time, in the salon of a respectable and cold woman, in the company of her friends, and suddenly, without warning, that is, I mean to say, completely unexpectedly, such an intimate gesture! She jumped like a tiger. She forgot herself completely. The woman in her was awakened, probably for the first time in her life. She shrieked and with a quick movement slapped my face. I don't know what would have happened if we'd been alone! What the animated marble of her body wasn't capable of! That vile character, Stok or Strok, came to her rescue. He began to yell: 'Young man, you're an old man, but you're acting like a little boy!' And he threw me out of the house.

"We haven't met since then. But I know she'll never forget that moment. And I know she'll avoid encounters with me. The poor thing! But you've grown quiet, my dear girl. You're afraid of me. You don't have to be afraid of Vovochka!"

He did his "cutie" number, pursing his lips in a Cupid's bow and blinking his eyes. "Vovochka ith a thweetie."

"Stop it," Lizochka said with annoyance. "People are looking at us."

"Does it really matter, if we love each other? Ach, women, women! You're all the same. You know what Turgenev said, I mean Dostoevsky—you know, that famous dramatist and expert. 'You must astonish a woman.' Oh, how true that is! My last affair . . . I astonished her. I threw money about like a madman and was humble as a madonna. I sent her a proper bouquet of carnations. Then a huge box of candy—a pound and a half, with a bow. And then, once she was intoxicated with her power and regarded me as her slave, I suddenly stopped pursuing her. You can imagine what that did to her nerves! All this madness, flowers, candy, anticipated evenings at the Paramount Theater and suddenly—*finis*! I waited a day, two days. And then the doorbell rings. I just knew it! It's her. She comes in pale, trembling . . . 'I've just come for a minute,' she says. I take her face in both my palms and say powerfully but still—out of delicacy—inquiringly: 'Are you mine?'

"She pushed me aside . . ."

"And slapped your face?" Lizochka asked in an automatic way.

"Mm . . . not exactly. She quickly took control of herself. As an experienced woman she understood what suffering was awaiting her. She recoiled and, with blanched lips, babbled: 'Give me two hundred forty eight francs until Tuesday, please.' "

"Well, and then?" asked Lizochka.

"Well, and nothing."

"You gave her the money?"

"I did."

"What happened then?"

"She took the money and left. I never saw her again."

"She never gave the money back?" Lizochka asked, surprised.

"What a child you are!" Gutbrecht laughed. "You know, she took the money only so that she could justify her visit to me. She took hold of herself and snapped that fiery thread which stretched between us. And I understand completely why she avoids meeting me. You know, there are limits even to her strengths. Yes, my dear child, what a dark abyss of voluptuousness I've opened before your frightened eyes. Oh, what an amazing woman she was! What an extraordinary passion!"

Lizochka fell to thinking. "Maybe . . ." she said. "But in my opinion, you would have been better off with another slap on the face. They're more practical."

What We Weren't Told About Faust

He dreamed that he stood once again before Mephistopheles and incanted:

*"Ach, gib mir wieder jene Triebe
Das tiefe Schmerzenfolle Glück.
Des Hasses Kraft, die Macht der Liebe,
Gib mein Jugend mir zurück."*

"Give me happiness, full of pain! Give me the strength of hatred! Give me the power of love! Return to me my youth!"

The dream was unsettling, but for the first time in many years Faust slept till ten o'clock.

He woke up, stretched, and noted with surprise that his back didn't ache.

With an habitual movement he grabbed himself by the chin to pull his long, scraggly grey beard out from under the blanket. He grabbed for it and froze. There was no beard. His short thick locks were curly. He jumped up, sat down, brought his legs down from the bed, and remembered everything.

"I'm young!"

And he felt ravenous for breakfast.

In his cupboard he found half a bottle of sour milk and a small dried rusk. This was the usual breakfast he permitted himself at six o'clock in the morning after a long night of laboratory work.

But in a second he'd already swallowed the milky, sour-tasting stuff, crunched the rusk, and clicked his tongue. "Not enough!"

He thought for a minute and went into the other room, where his pupil worked during the day.

"Wagner," he recalled, "is always chewing on something. He probably has some food hidden here."

Groping in all the corners, he found a large chunk of sausage and a piece of pumpernickel bread behind a jar with the homunculus.

"It would be nice to have something to drink with this," he muttered, confused by such an atypical thought in his brain. "Beer would be good!"

But there was no beer. Faust's eyes came to rest on the jar with the homunculus. There was alcohol in the jar.

Once again a strange and unusual thought rose up in his mind. He remembered how the neighborhood schoolboys had once gotten into his laboratory and drunk up the alcohol from under a toad's heart, which he'd intended for an experimental union with a black lily.

"Those boys were satisfied, even though Wagner thrashed them."

The recollections suddenly stopped as Faust returned to reality. He burst the bubble which had been corked up in the homunculus bottle and drank the liquid down. He wheezed and thrust his teeth into the sausage: "Bliss!"

He was about to cry, "Stop this moment!" when he remembered that that was precisely what he could no longer do. He shook his head, laughed, finished the sausage, and went to get dressed.

Here he noticed with some irritation that his gown was about to split along the seams. As a youth, he had become larger and heavier. But somehow he managed to pull it on. He seized his hat and was about to grab his cane when he realized that he no longer needed it. Faust went out into the street. He remembered that he had to drop in at the old alchemist's to explain to him the union of the Lion with the Amethyst, but suddenly the alchemist, the Lion and the Amethyst seemed completely beside the point. His plan to go to a beer hall seemed much more urgent.

"I'm young!" he exulted. "Now life will give me what I wanted, what I sold my soul to the devil for. 'Happiness deep as pain, the strength of hatred, the power of love . . . youth.'"

He walked to the beer hall.

"I, the old doctor Faust, know that I ought to go visit the alchemist, and here I am going to a beer hall. It's my foolish youth stirring me up. And I can't do a thing about it! Have I really become so lazy? How strange and wicked."

But he continued to act strangely and wickedly anyway. He entered the beer hall.

There were already a lot of people there. In order to get a seat he had to use cunning. He seized a moment when one comfortable little old man got up to greet his friends. Faust quickly took his seat. The little old man returned, was insulted, and began to grumble.

"Yes," another old man supported him. "Young people these days are not only rude, but downright insolent. Look, young man," he turned to Faust, "in our time a youth not only did not allow himself to take an elderly person's seat, but on the contrary, would give up his own."

"You should be ashamed, young man," grumbled the first old man. "What will become of you when you're old? A lazy-bones is what you'll turn into—an idler, an ignoramus, and a smart aleck."

"An ignoramus?" Faust was surprised. "I'm a doctor. A philosopher."

"Ha-ha-ha-ha-ha!" Everyone around burst into laughter, all at one time.

"What a joker!"

"He's drunk!"

"How dissipated our youth has become! Instead of studying and working, they sit in beer halls from morning on."

"And create scandals."

"And lie."

"He needs some beer poured down the back of his shirt," someone suggested.

"Well, I don't advise touching him. He's a healthy fellow."

Faust looked around at the eyes of those present. All the faces were mocking, unfriendly.

"Will I have to fight?"

He didn't know whether he was strong or weak. Out of agitation he forgot that he was young and hurried to leave the tavern.

It was a cheerful day outside, sunny and bright. From around a corner a drum boomed. Soldiers passed by. Faust admired their strong, courageous figures, their youthful step, their sturdy legs.

"Oh, if only my youth would return!" he sighed by force of habit.

"Why are you loafing around here?" an old woman snapped at him. "Why aren't you going to the front? Look, good sirs, at this strapping young fellow standing and idly chattering! He doesn't want to defend his country."

"You should be ashamed, young man," said a respectable passerby. "You're not going to fight and now you've insulted an old lady."

"He looks suspicious to me," someone piped up. "He's dressed up like a petty official."

"That's true," another affirmed. "His gown wasn't made for him—he's wearing an old man's caftan. He obviously robbed some old man."

"They should arrest him and send him away."

"There's no question about it. It's clear that he's an undesirable foreigner."

A guard with a halberd approached.

"Did you catch this fellow?" he asked the crowd.

"Yes, we caught him."

"Well, then, let's go to the police station."

The guard grabbed Faust by the back of his collar.

"They'll send him off to the front," the people in the crowd said.

"Oh youth, youth, how dissipated it has become!"

" '*Des Hasses Kraft*—the strength of hatred,' " Faust recalled.

He tried as best he could to get away. Suddenly he drew his arm back and slugged the guard in the jaw.

"Well done, the devil take him!" he loudly cried.

"Take him?" echoed a familiar voice. "I'll take him!"

Over Faust's shoulder smiled the dear familiar face of Mephistopheles.

"I'll take him!" repeated Mephistopheles.

"Let him go now, dearie," he said to the guard. "He's my friend."

He stooped over and whispered something in the guard's ear. The guard grinned, stared at the devil with surprise, and let Faust go.

Mephistopheles took Faust by the hand and led him calmly along the street.

"Where are we going?" asked Faust.

"To loaf around," answered the devil. "Young people always loaf around. Let's go over there, they're dancing on the square. Soon you'll meet Margarita."

****

"Margarita! Margarita! Margarita!" Faust muttered angrily, striding about his laboratory. "It goes without saying that the devil palmed her off on me."

The laboratory was foul, dark and dusty. Wagner had made off long ago.

"I was an obedient pupil of the wise doctor Faust," Wagner explained. "But what could I do with this passionate lad who reeks of beer from morning till night and talks about nothing but girls? I have too much respect for myself to remain here."

He seized the black cat, the white rooster, the magic wand, and left.

"The devil has turned out to be a real idiot," Faust complained. "You know what he imagines? He imagines that in me, the young Faust, an old man's tastes have remained. That a young, rosy calf like Margarita is the be-all and end-all for me. What a fool! The devil's cunning enough in general, but as far as sensuality goes—what a bungler! I'm a young man now, I don't need what that slobbering old Doctor Faust dreamed about. I need a clever coquette, a bea-u-tiful countess, someone cruel and bright who'll make me giddy and turn my head. Someone who'd torment me. As for Gretchen, she's the same sour milk I used to drink in the morning."

He stopped, listening to himself.

"How strange! With youth, all my thoughts have become simple and utterly clear. All my learning has remained intact. I haven't forgotten a thing, yet somehow it's all much simpler."

The boom of a drum and shouts carried up from the street.

"The soldiers are marching. Strange—I want to work a bit in my laboratory, but the sound of the drum lures me to march. O-one-two! . . . It's humiliating! And this vile appetite of mine, this passionate interest in food and drink. Not an epicurean interest, as old people have—mushrooms, a bit of wine, a piece of chicken, something sour. No. Mine is a robust interest, voracious and raging. A cheerful interest, too. My whole being is happy, it shines and sparkles from fried sausage with beer."

Faust sat down and laid his head on his hands. Calming down, he grew sad.

"The devil has humiliated me. It's a low-down trick. I should never have indulged myself, I should have talked myself out of it. But there's nothing to be done now. I'll just have to go to Margarita and enjoy the Eternal Feminine. I'll pick up a brooch for her . . ."

"Devil, dearie," Faust said to Mephistopheles several days later. "Gretchen is charming. Although I myself chose her, I suspect now that it's you who palmed her off on me. But here (as they'll say several centuries from now), here I observe an inconsistency. And the more I think about it, the less I understand it. Why did you order a whole box of trinkets sent to her? She was supposed to lose her head over me *without* the help of earrings. I'm young and healthy. To my way of thinking, you've messed things up for me. Old men need earrings. But I have the *Macht der Liebe*, the power of love. Why earrings, then? It's humiliating. Why don't you answer me? He's silent. So now I'm beginning to doubt the power of love. That doesn't fit into my plans at all. What did I sell my soul for, then? What did we struggle for? He's silent. And then, dearie, there's one more delicate point. Yes, I'm young. My body, really, is only twenty years old. But you know (between you and me, of course) my soul turned seventy-six the day before yesterday. You have to take that into consideration. I'm bored . . . Margarita of course is a darling, a cupcake, pure charm. But, you know (this is also between you and me), she's a perfect fool. For example, last night we were sitting together in the garden. The roses were fragrant. Oh, those eternal flowers! How the head spins from them . . . Dawn would soon be breaking and the nightingale had fallen silent. How wonderful is this sweet languour of the young, strong body! Like the nightingale, it has sung its pre-dawn song and is slumbering among the lilacs. It dozes. But the soul does not sleep. The soul, as it were, has freed itself from the power of the body, from the *schmerzenfolle Glück*, and sunk deep into its innermost sanctum. I began to talk about the laboratory, about the philosopher's stone. But Gretchen—she's a dear girl, of course, she'd dried some pumpkin seeds—she just sat and shelled them! Well, what could I do, Devil? I was bored! To run back to the laboratory seemed awkward and silly. She'd see that I'm a fool. I desired, I sobbed, I placed my soul at stake. Devil! Be a decent demon! Return my grey beard to me! Return to me my golden old age!"

Iago

We all know that there are in the world both nice people and nasty ones. And we make this distinction no matter whether they harm us or help us.

A nice person can wrap you around his finger and use his niceness to his own advantage, so that later you're amazed at how you could swallow the line of such a scoundrel.

But to defend ourselves, we scatter-brains have our so-called reputations. We are forewarned and forearmed against certain "nice" individuals. After all, we know that certain people can play an important role in our lives, so we are always on guard against people we don't know well or haven't studied. If we do swallow their lines, we are ourselves partly to blame.

But in relation to *things*, we're totally defenseless. Maybe the idea of relating to things seems strange. How can inanimate objects relate? Precisely because we don't understand how they can, we're defenseless against them.

Who hasn't heard the legend about diamonds that bring misfortune to all who possess them? People talk about diamonds only because they're valuable and precious—it's even romantic to suffer because of them. No one's going to talk about some frying pan falling out of a kitchen cupboard and crippling two housecats with a single blow. That's petty. Kitchens, cats, frying pans—what kind of topics are they for conversation!

But let's put the frying pans aside for now. Let's move on to a more fashionable subject.

Every woman knows there are lucky dresses and unlucky ones. A lucky dress can be one that doesn't make much of an impression, that's old or even unbecoming, but whenever you put it on, you feel happy and content—everything turns out successfully, everyone is kind and affectionate.

An unlucky dress can be charming, expensive, and very attractive, it can fit like a glove, awakening delight and envy. But once you put it on you're sorry you're alive. The man you've put it on for either doesn't show up at the party at all, or if he does, he displays utter indifference, even hostility. And you have no idea why.

A woman wearing an unlucky dress will feel bored, offended and lonely, unneeded by anyone. And feeling this way, she'll become awkward, unimaginative, vapid, genuinely unhappy.

And this will happen every time she puts on the dress.

Of course, psychologists would explain it this way: the first time the woman wears the dress, she doesn't have a good time. Consequently, every time she puts it on, she feels anxious, subconsciously expecting a replay of unpleasant experiences. This anxiety depresses her, makes her awkward and unsure of herself, and thus dull company.

I can attest that this analysis is untrue. A woman who has paid a fortune for a dress and considers it becoming would never admit, even in her subconscious, that it's because of the dress she's having a bad time. Long, and conscious, experience is required before she'll conclude, "You know, every time I put on my charming dress, failure awaits me." Such a conclusion would cause a catastrophe: she'd have to throw her dress away.

There can also be "unlucky" accessories to the total effect—watches, rings, and makeup can also be unlucky.

****

Now it sometimes happens that a rather cumbersome piece of furniture is introduced into an apartment, ruining the life of those living there, setting them at odds, dividing them, tattling, slandering. And no one would ever imagine that a cursed sofa was to blame.

For example, my friend had a mirrored wardrobe. It had the most ordinary walnut exterior. Inside it was divided by a vertical partition, with hooks on the right side for dresses and shelves on the left for linens and such. It was so ordinary, I'm embarrassed to describe it.

And can you possibly imagine that this harmless-looking wardrobe was capable of playing the role of informer, spy, traitor—of a Shakespearian Iago?

The wardrobe stood in the bedroom. Since the apartment was done in the modern style, the bedroom had no door—it was joined to the living room by a large archway. The wardrobe stood along the middle of the bedroom wall. Directly across from it, on the living room wall, was another mirror, hung crookedly, yet cunningly, so that no matter where you went, you were reflected in the wardrobe mirror.

My friend's husband was a busy man. He would come home at the most unpredictable hours, unlocking the door with his key. And the first thing to confront him was always the mirrored reflection of whatever was going on in the apartment. The clever mirror even managed to catch what was going on in the dining room and the hall by reflecting off the narrow mirror over the buffet. Like a gossip and a spy, the wardrobe ran ahead of everyone to greet the master of the house; rushing and garbling things, it reported everything.

His wife would try in vain to convince him that the wardrobe mirror distorted things.

"Who was sneaking along the hall to the back staircase?" the husband might ask darkly.

"Why, no one at all!" the wife would answer, nobly indignant. "Go look, there's no one there. You're crazy!"

"Why bother looking?" the husband persisted. "You think he's waiting for me so I can slug him in the mouth?"

Under various pretexts the wife tried to move the wardrobe. But then its mirror would wink into the hall. It was impossible to hide from it, even in the bathroom.

More loathsome than anything, according to the innocent victim (or rather, sufferer), was the fact that the wardrobe lied. It reflected things which never occurred.

"Don't you see?" she would say. "It's like a mirage in the desert. There are plenty of optical and auditory illusions in the world, not to mention other kinds."

The wardrobe deceived with the "other kinds."

One day, returning home, the owner of the wardrobe saw in its mirror his wife, lying in a graceful pose on the couch in the embraces of a gentleman.

The wardrobe's owner stepped into the room and saw that next to his wife was sitting Doctor Ferezev, their regular doctor. The doctor, most likely, had just listened to his wife's lungs, because a stethoscope, devised for that purpose, was lying right there on the table.

The wife was silent, her eyes wide. But the doctor, with unnatural delight, began to exclaim: "And here's our husband! And here's our husband!"

He repeated it over and over, faster and sillier, until the amazed husband asked his wife: "Are you sick?"

To which his wife replied, inappropriately, in an offended tone: "Why are you always carping? The doctor says I have a cough."

Actually, the husband had no reason to be surprised or suspicious. The doctor had dropped in and found a cough. Up to that moment there had been no cough, but that's a doctor's job—to seek out the hidden evil. He searched for it and found it. What the wardrobe reflected was nonsense. It foreshortened the image, and the result was an affront to marital honor. Of course, it did seem strange that the doctor, instead of greeting the husband in a normal manner, began to shriek like a parrot. But you can't seriously blame him for that. Especially since his exclamations were jovial and, so to speak, welcoming. If the doctor had gotten himself into a compromising situation, he would most likely have begun to shout, "The devil take it,"—and without such enthusiasm, you can be sure. At least that's what the husband thought, so the matter passed smoothly.

But the wardrobe thought otherwise.

About two weeks after this incident, the husband, returning home, was struck by the reflection of his wife, who was this time standing in the middle of the room. An innocent pose, except she wasn't standing alone. Some unknown character was embracing her and, if the wardrobe were to be believed, kissing her right on the lips. At that moment the wife turned her head, and her eyes appeared in the mirror. At first they were their usual size and shape, but little by little they grew round and bulging. Suddenly she turned away and, pushing aside the character, whispered: "We'd better start the phonograph, or else we've had it."

The character began to cackle strangely. Then shifting his gaze, he too met another pair of eyes in the mirror—which he obviously did not expect. He stopped short.

"Is that you, Vasya?" the wife called in a perfectly natural tone. "Would you start the phonograph, dear? Monsieur Pirozhnikov has kindly agreed to show me a new dance step."

Well, the wardrobe had lied again. Again it had contrived foreshortenings and made a fool of him and his suspicions.

Monsieur Pirozhnikov turned out to be an idiot and a boor to boot. Without a word he took his hat, bowed, and left. As if he had been chased out.

"He's shy and not too bright," the wife explained.

She'd never fall for a type like that, of course.

That storm, too, passed over, but the wardrobe still wouldn't settle down. It played such mean tricks—only a human would be capable of them. And not just any human, only a vengeful and furious one. An Iago.

(Incidentally, why does everyone attack Iago so venomously? Shakespeare clearly alludes to a flirtation between Othello and Iago's wife. Consequently Iago, by destroying the Moor's happiness, is taking revenge out of jealousy. He, then, was also an Othello.)

But let's get back to the wardrobe.

The wardrobe was worse than Iago. No one had affronted *its* marital honor, and it was not suffering from jealousy. But this is what it did:

One day the husband, in his wife's absence, was looking for his necktie. Not finding it after a long search, he decided that his wife had put it in her wardrobe.

Iago

Cursing his wife for her disorderliness, he yanked at the mirrored door, and at that very moment, from the upper shelf, a packet tied with a flimsy ribbon came flying out, smacking him on the forehead and showering him with letters.

"Here, you fool," the wardrobe seemed to say. "You have to be hit in the head to believe it."

The wardrobe's victim sat on the floor for a long time, reading the letters written in various hands:

"... I'll come when your idiot isn't home..."

"... I know that you're burning with passion—I am burning too..."

"... what can be more blissful than your embraces..."

"... I love when you whisper 'more, more'..."

The victim read on, wondering with bewilderment and some curiosity: "Who's this one from? And this one?"

And the wardrobe triumphantly reflected his face—miserable and foolish.